The paper was we... ... the snow, and the pencil writing faint; Kate stood under a street light and squinted at the words through her crooked glasses.

'It's a list!' she called excitedly to Desmond. 'It could be the one, you know! It could be!' She peered closer at the paper. 'It says *telly*!' she squealed. 'Desmond! It says *telly*!'

That proved it, of course! Jacob's telly had been stolen, the word *telly* was on this paper – what else could the paper be but the burglar's list? Dropped in haste yesterday, as he fled from the scene of his crime. Excitement cleaved its way upwards, slicing through Kate's chest; excitement so sharp that it hurt. With shining eyes she turned to call at Desmond once more.

She was just in time to see him heave his stone through the front window of Jacob's house.

GUILTY!

Ruth Thomas

RED FOX

F 12805

My thanks to Richard Handford for the idea, and
to Caroline Roberts for invaluable help and advice.

A Red Fox Book

Published by Random House Children's Books
20 Vauxhall Bridge Road, London SW1V 2SA

A division of Random House UK Ltd
London Melbourne Sydney Auckland
Johannesburg and agencies throughout the world

First published in 1993 by Hutchinson Children's Books

Red Fox edition 1993

3 5 7 9 10 8 6 4

Printed and bound in Great Britain by
Cox & Wyman Ltd, Reading, Berkshire

RANDOM HOUSE UK Limited Reg. No. 954009

ISBN 0 09 918591 1

To my great-niece, Kate Nicholas

1

Burglars!

Someone was crying. The sobs penetrated closed windows and bunched net curtains, adding grief to the biting cold of the London street. 'Listen!' said Kate. 'There's somebody crying!'

Desmond had found a piece of wood in the gutter which was great for rapping on people's gateposts and things. He gave another satisfying smack to the boundary wall of Jacob's house. 'There's somebody crying,' said Kate again, in a troubled voice. 'It sounds like Jacob.'

'All right, all right,' said Desmond, without turning round. 'I'm not deaf!'

'Poor little Jacob, though,' said Kate, peering over the wall, and chewing a piece of hair.

'It's only his mum thumped him, innit?'

'Desmond! You know Jacob's mum ain't home yet!'

'So what?'

'So I'm going to see what he's crying for,' said Kate. 'You coming?'

'. . . Ah-h-h – I suppose so.'

A black nose and a white one pressed against the bay window. 'It's all messy in there,' said Kate, mystified. 'All the drawers and things, on the floor.'

'Been burglared, innit?' said Desmond, not looking at her.

Desmond was touchy on the subject of burglary. His dad had only recently come out of prison, and already people in the street were accusing him of things he hadn't done. Desmond would like to beat up the people who were accusing his dad of things he hadn't done. He would like to smash their faces in, and hurt them, and hurt them . . . . Liars! Liars!

Desmond peered through the letterbox.

Jacob was sitting in the dark hall, bawling his heart out. He was still in his outdoor clothes, his anorak fully zipped, the hood still covering the tight black curls. 'Get up!' called Desmond. 'And open the door!'

'I'm *scared*!'

'Open the door!' said Desmond, grimly, thumping on it with his piece of wood.

The door moved, just a fraction. 'Come on, come on!' said Desmond. 'How we supposed to see you, hiding behind there?'

The eight-year-old face, deep in the shadows of the hood, was streaked and grimy with tears. Great brown eyes looked piteously from one to the other of the older children. 'They took all our things,' he wailed. 'They took the *telly*!'

'Did you tell the police?' said Kate. She was conscious, somewhere at the back of her mind, that the Secret Seven, in similar circumstances, would most likely get on with solving the crime themselves; but she couldn't think, for the moment, how they usually set about it.

The head in its hood turned from side to side.

'You *didn't* tell the police?'

The head turned again.

'Can I, then? Can I?' Behind the glasses, lopsided on her nose as usual, Kate's eyes gleamed. From somewhere near the pit of her stomach a little knot of excitement swelled, and grew, and spread quickly

2

through all of her, so there was nowhere the
excitement didn't reach. 'Let me! Let me!'

'I want my mum!' wailed Jacob.

'Your mum's going to come soon. She is, Jacob,
don't cry . . . . Oh, let me phone! Let me dial 999!'
Kate hopped up and down, desperate with anxiety
that someone else might do it first. 'Have you got
a phone in your house?'

'Something wrong?' said the lady next door,
coming in with her basket on wheels.

'There's burglars been in my house,' sobbed
Jacob.

'Oh, my God!' screamed the lady next door. She
screamed it again, and again.

A small crowd began to gather. Most of them
had come out of their houses to see what the screaming was about. They stood without coats, hugging
their arms and stamping their feet, and sucking the
bitter air through their teeth. A moment before, the
street had been practically deserted; now there were
half a dozen people outside Jacob's house, all talking at once, taking over.

'What a shame.'

'Where does your mum work, Jacob?'

'Oh, my God!'

'What did they take?'

'How did they get in, then?'

'What a shame.'

Mrs Harris hobbled across the road with her
amiable mongrel dog. Mrs Harris's eyes were
gleaming, and Bruce's tongue lolled expectantly.
Something was going on, and Mrs Harris and Bruce
weren't going to miss it, not likely!

'Another break-in.'

'Never!' said Mrs Harris, trying not to sound as

3

though she was enjoying herself, which she was. And Bruce pushed through the circle, wagging his tail to show that whatever all this was about, he was in it too. He rubbed his nose against Kate's hand, thrusting and squealing until she bent to give him his customary cuddle.

'What a shame.'

'Has anybody phoned the police?'

'I'll do that,' said Mrs Harris, eagerly. 'I'll do that, I'll do that!' It really was her day.

I knew it, Kate thought, watching her go. I just knew that was going to happen. It's not fair, it wasn't that old nuisance's burglary, it was mine. Well . . . mine and Desmond's. We found it, not her.

The disappointment was intense. Behind Mrs Harris's retreating back, Kate made a face. And since the face she already had was far from beautiful, the one she made for Mrs Harris was hideous indeed.

'I'm going home,' said Desmond, suddenly.

'Shan't we wait and see the police cars come?' said Kate, disappointed again. She didn't want to watch them by herself, she wanted someone to enjoy it all with her.

'Nah!' Desmond's expression was sullen, guarded. He did not trust the police; he had been taught from his earliest years not to.

'Come on,' Kate wheedled, not understanding.

'Belt up, Frog.'

'Don't call me that!'

'Belt up, then, like I said.'

'Oh, belt up yourself!'

They walked in silence as far as Kate's house. 'I wish Bruce was *my* dog,' said Kate.

Desmond grunted.

4

'I said I wish Bruce was my dog,' said Kate.

'All right, all right, I heard.'

''Bye, then. See you tomorrow,' said Kate, without resentment.

Desmond grunted, and shrugged, and went.

A police car rounded the corner. It sped up the road, and Kate fell over her feet to get indoors. 'Guess what? Guess what?'

Her dad and her sister were in the sitting room, glued to the television as usual. 'I found a burglary,' said Kate.

'Shut up,' said Dawn, fretfully. 'Can't you see we're trying to watch? And close that door, it's freezing in here!'

'You know Doctor said I got to keep warm,' Dad reproached her.

Dad, stretched out on the sofa and wrapped in blankets, coughed and wheezed and coughed again. His eyes streamed, and the thin sandy hair was limp, tired-looking. 'You made his cough worse,' said Dawn. 'You let the draught in.'

'I found a burglary,' said Kate. 'Up the road.'

'All right.' Dawn was unimpressed. 'You told us once.'

'Second break-in this week,' said Dad, drawing his breath in sharply and noisily after the last word.

'Third!' said Dawn.

'Yeah, right. . . . Don't know what we have police for!'

'Anyway, I *found* this one,' said Kate. 'Doesn't anybody think it's exciting?'

Another bout of coughing filled the room with painful, tearing sound. 'Get him a drink of water, Kate,' said Dawn. 'Or how about make us a cup of tea?'

'Why not you?' said Kate.

'It's too hard to get up. With this lump. You got no idea how heavy it is.'

The 'lump' was Dawn's baby, due to be born at the end of next month. The lump was certainly enormous, swelling like some huge inflated balloon, stretching out the blue spots of Dawn's maternity dress. The lump filled Dawn's thoughts, as well as her stomach. She deplored it, and boasted about it, endlessly.

'Do you know something?' said Kate.

'What?'

'I'm sick of hearing about your lump.'

Dawn shrugged. There was a smug little smile on her pretty pink and white face.

'Don't be like that, Kate,' said Dad, coughing and retching all over the place again.

In the tiny kitchen, with the paint peeling off the walls, Kate put the kettle on the gas stove. There was a pile of dirty cups and plates in the sink; Kate washed them while she waited for the kettle. Mum will be tired when she comes home, Kate thought. If I wash the dishes Mum will say what a good girl I am . . . perhaps.

She put the mugs, with the tea bags in them, on a tray. I'm going to make this tea really good, Kate thought. I'm going to make this tea really, *really* good. Dad is going to say this is the best cup of tea he ever had. I think.

'Bit weak!' Dad complained. 'Not so much sugar next time.'

Kate sighed, and tried again. 'You know that burglary I found—'

'Shush!' said Dawn. 'We're trying to watch telly.'

'Why?' said Kate. 'It's boring.'

'Shush!' said Dawn.

Kate took *Good Work Secret Seven* out of her school bag; but there was nowhere comfortable to sit, since Dad was taking up the whole of the sofa, and Dawn was in the one armchair. That left only the hard chairs round the dining table. 'Can I go in the bedroom, Dawn, and get in your bed?' said Kate.

'No.'

'Why not?'

'Because it's private for me and Frank now. Now we're married it's private for me and Frank. It's not your bedroom any more.'

'It's not really fair, though.'

'Don't be like that, Kate,' said Dad.

'She keeps on and on at me about it,' said Dawn.

'Don't be like that, Kate,' said Dad, again. 'It's only till the Council find them a place.'

'I wish the Council weren't so slow,' said Kate. 'There's nowhere for *me* to be private. And the telly is too loud.'

'Go and get in our bed,' said Dad.

'I don't want to.'

'Go on – your mum won't mind.'

'I don't *want* to.' She couldn't get into Dad's bed, Kate thought, she just couldn't. Dad's bed was full of bronchitis; it smelled of vapour rub, and medicine. 'I want my half of the back bedroom, like before.'

'Well you can't' said Dawn. 'Not till the Council find a place for me and Frank.'

'I could sleep upstairs. Mr Duffy got three rooms upstairs, all to himself. I think Mr Duffy's greedy.'

'You can't talk like that!' said Dad, scandalized. 'This is Mr Duffy's house.'

'I'm going to ask Mr Duffy if I can have one of

7

his rooms for my bedroom.' Kate moved towards the door. What a good idea she'd just had! Why hadn't anybody thought of that before?

'You're not doing no such thing!' said Dad, thoroughly alarmed. His voice wheezed, and rose in pitch to a squeal. 'Do you want to get us all throwed out?'

'You said Mr Duffy ain't allowed to throw us out.'

'He can if we do something wrong. What if he gets us for overcrowding, then? What about that? He might, you know, if he thinks of it. You don't want to go and put the idea in his head!'

Dad was Mr Duffy's sitting tenant. First Dad's dad was the tenant, and then Dad was. Dad had been born in this house, and he intended to die in it. His greatest fear was that Mr Duffy, whom they hardly ever saw, whom they sometimes forgot was even there, might nevertheless one day find a loophole in the law that said the ground floor of Number 58 Wessex Road was Dad's home for life.

Kate stood by the door, and chewed a piece of her long, straggly hair. She wrinkled her nose, too small to hold the glasses properly, and the glasses bounced up and down. She wrinkled it faster to see if she could actually make the glasses fall off. She stuck out her underlip and squinted at it, down the side of her nose.

'Your *face*!' said Dawn, disparagingly.

'What's wrong with my face?'

'We don't like looking at it, that's what!'

Dad coughed and coughed, his eyes were bloodshot, and his face bright red with the strain. The coughing hurt Kate too; she could feel it in her chest every time he did it. Her fingers scrabbled at the door handle.

'Where you going? You're making Dad worse. You're letting the cold air in.'

'Outside,' said Kate. 'Where you can't see my face you don't like looking at.'

'Don't let her go upstairs, Dawnie,' Dad begged, pathetic in his anxiety.

'If you go upstairs, our mum's going to belt you!' Dawn threatened.

Kate stood in the draughty hall and thought about her face. She knew she had a funny sort of face. Dawn was the pretty one, and she was the funny one; Kate knew that. And what could you do with a funny face except make it worse, for a joke? Fancy anybody thinking she was going to go upstairs, though, after Dad explained why she mustn't! Even if it *was* still hard to understand how it could be right for Mr Duffy to have three whole rooms to himself when she couldn't even have half of one.

Anyway, she wasn't going to sleep on that blow-up bed in the sitting room any more, she just decided it.

So where, then? Where was she going to sleep?

How about under the stairs? Now there was another idea nobody'd thought of yet! Kate opened the door that led to under the stairs and peered in. The cupboard was dark, and full. There was the Hoover, and the steps, and the ironing board; and right inside, where the roof was low, was a multitude of cardboard boxes and plastic bags.

Kate threw out the Hoover and the steps and the ironing board, and they clattered any old how over the lino in the hall. 'Are you smashing up the house or what?' called Dawn. Kate tugged at heavy card-board boxes. 'Our mum's going to kill you!' called Dawn. Kate threw out the last of the plastic bags, and a sunny smile lit up the funny sort of face. It was going to be a *dear* little bedroom.

The clutter from the cupboard blocked the narrow hall. Kate climbed over the mountain she had erected, and peeked around the sitting room door again, beaming through the crooked glasses.

'You know what's going to happen when Mum comes home, don't you?' said Dawn, turning in her chair and moving the lump carefully with her hands.

That was a point – there might be a big row to come! Not necessarily, though; you couldn't always tell, with Mum, which way she was going to go.

'If you been and made a mess out there,' said Dad, 'if you made a mess out there, your mum's going to have the hide off of you!'

'I'm only making a bedroom,' said Kate.

'Where?'

'Under the stairs, where do you think?'

'I think you gone off your trolley,' said Dawn.

Kate dragged her inflatable bed from its place behind the sofa in the sitting room, and into the cupboard under the stairs. She went back for the new duvet they had bought her, to make up for not having a bedroom any more. She lay on the blow-up bed, and covered herself with the duvet because there was no central heating. And after all, she discovered, she couldn't actually read because there was no light. But it was private in there, and it was all hers! It was better than the bedroom she used to share with Dawn, even. It was Kate's Place. It was *wonderful*.

There was a rattling of keys at the front door. Inside the sitting room Dawn and Dad looked at each other, and braced themselves. 'Wait for it!' said Dad.

'There she goes!' said Dawn, covering her lump with protective hands.

The old house trembled and quailed under the fury of Mum's tongue-lashing. 'What's all this, then? World War Three started, has it? Pity nobody bothered to tell me, I could have fetched home my gas mask! . . . Come on out the one that done it, and they better have a good answer!'

'Hope old Duffy ain't got his hearing aid in,' Dad whispered, to Dawn.

Mum threw open the sitting room door. 'Well? Everybody lost their tongue? Everybody forgot how to speak the English language?'

'It wasn't us,' said Dawn, faintly. 'It was Kate.'

'Oh? What's the matter with you two, then? You grown roots out of your bums or something? You couldn't get up and stop her?'

'I told her,' said Dawn. 'She wouldn't take no notice.'

Dad coughed, and coughed, and coughed. 'Don't make out worse than you are!' Mum scolded him, in her laser-sharp voice. 'And I believe *you'd* go on sitting there if the house was falling down! Yeah – it's you I'm talking to, Madam Dawn, or should I say Lady Muck? It won't do you no harm to shift yourself once in a while, you know. You ain't the first girl ever had a baby. What give you the idea to put your feet up a whole two months? Something special about you? It's heavier for you than it is for anybody else? I went out to work to the last minutes before having you, I might tell you!'

11

Mum looked as though she never put her feet up, ever. Her face was thin, and yellowish, and lined; and her eyes were muddy pools of worry.

'Frank don't want me to strain myself, does he?' said Dawn. 'And anyway I've got a pain today,' she added, untruthfully.

'Where's Kate?' said Mum, ignoring that.

'In here,' said Kate, in a small voice, from under the stairs.

'Come on out!'

'It *is* a dear little bedroom,' said Kate sadly, crawling into the hall.

'Put all them things back where they was before. Go on!'

'It would have been a dear little bedroom though!'

'Yeah – well you're getting a dear little thump if you don't hurry up with turning it back into a cupboard.'

She *had* made rather a mess, now she came to notice it. Kate was truly sorry about the mess. Poor Mum, seeing all that mess when she came in tired from work. 'I found a burglary today,' Kate said, heaving away at the boxes again.

'Never mind burglary!'

'Up the road.'

'Get on with it, get on with it! I don't suppose neither of you two layabouts in there thought about something to eat tonight. . . . No, of course not! This is a hotel, this is! Everybody supposed to sit around and wait for the staff to serve them!'

'Doctor did say I got to keep warm.' Dad clutched his blankets around him, and ventured a reproachful glance at the still-open door.

'He said you supposed to move around an' all, so don't give me that!'

'I was going to start the tea but I got this pain,' said Dawn. 'Perhaps it's the baby, coming early.'

'More likely rigor mortis setting in!' said Mum.

'*I* did the washing up,' said Kate.

'Well now you can lay the table,' said Mum.

In the kitchen, today's cooking smells began to overlay yesterday's. Kate rooted for knives and forks. 'Can we have a dog?' said Kate.

'No.' said Mum.

'It would be nice if we could.'

'It would be nice if Princess Di come to tea. But she ain't coming this week. So far as I know.'

'All right . . . . What about my burglary?'

'What about it?'

'It seems like nobody wants to listen.'

'Get on with it, then. What you waiting for?'

Kate was delighted. She didn't often get Mum's attention, because Mum was always so tired after work, and busy with other things. Kate beamed with pleasure. 'It was this boy in our school named Jacob. His house.'

'I know the one you mean. Up the top end.'

'That's right. Well – There was a burglary . . . . And it was me that found it!'

'Second break-in this week!' said Mum. 'No, no, I tell a lie. *Third* break-in. It's blimming disgusting! Course, we all know who's doing it.'

'Do we?'

'Yeah – that toe-rag down the road.'

'What toe-rag is that?'

'You know that friend of yours, that black boy, that grumpy little so and so. Whatsisname? Desmond.'

'He's not really my *friend*. He's just the boy I come home with after school, sometimes.'

'Same difference. Anyway, if you want to know who's been doing all this thieving, I'll bet any money you like, it's that boy's father.'

'Is it?'

'Just come out of prison for burglary, hasn't he! Three-four weeks ago.'

'*What*?'

'Don't tell me you didn't know!'

'Oh, yeah . . . I think I heard them say, but I forgot.'

'Well, there you are!'

Kate stood for several moments, digesting what she had just been told. 'I think it's terrible!' she said at last.

'It *is* terrible. I don't know what's happening to this country. Now we got to live with a thief in our own road!'

'I mean,' said Kate, 'I think it's terrible for Desmond. Poor Desmond! Poor old Desmond!'

'You don't want to go wasting your sympathy on them sort.'

'Don't I?'

'No, you don't! I wouldn't trust one of them Lockes no further than I could throw 'em! You save your sympathy for your own family. God knows we got enough problems. And we don't go breaking into other people's houses to solve them, neither.'

'Can't I be a *bit* sorry for Desmond, though?'

'You're going to be sorry for something in a minute, my girl. Put them eggs down you're playing with. Go on, put 'em down before you smash 'em. . . . And now get out the kitchen, you're more trouble here than you're worth! Go and see if your

14

dad wants another cup of tea. I don't like the sound of that cough, only don't tell him I said so. And go and see if Dawn's all right. She ain't really starting her baby, is she? That's all we need, if she is!'

Kate shuffled back to the sitting room, heel-to-toe all the way, taking a long time because she was thinking.

I know you're supposed to like the people in your family best, she thought. And I do, I think . . . I like my mum, most of the time . . . And I like my dad, some of the time . . . And I like Dawn, I suppose. . . . Well, she's my sister, isn't she, so I have to like her! . . . There's one person in my family I *really* like, though. There's one person I really, really like. And that person hasn't been in our family very long but I can't help about that, I still like him the best. . . . And he *is* in our family now, so it's all right to like him best, isn't it? And I'm longing for him to come home, I am, I'm just *longing* for that person to come home.

. . . And I don't believe it, I must be magic! I must be magic, because here he is, coming in the door now! 'Frank!' Kate exclaimed, joyfully. 'You're home!'

He came into the narrow hall, doubled up and staggering. 'Knackered,' he groaned. 'Absolutely knackered.'

'Poor Frank!' said Kate, indignantly. 'Did they make you work very hard today, then?'

He groaned again, but you could tell from his eyes that he was in high spirits.

'Yeah – they whipped the poor old horse today. Poor old horse!' He acted the part of the poor old horse, neighing and whinnying piteously; sometimes it seemed that Frank was only about ten and three-quarters – the same age as Kate. And Kate laughed, happier than she had been all day. Happier than she had been in the dear little bedroom, even! When Frank came into the house he brought the sun with him, even when there was no sun outside.

He stopped clowning and gave Kate a hug, so she felt warm and appreciated. 'How did it go today, then?'

'Great!' said Kate, looking up at Frank with a shining face. 'I found a burglary!'

'You never!'

'I did, then. Mum thinks the one that done it was Desmond Locke's dad. Because he just now come out of prison.'

'Most likely it *was* him, then. You got a pretty sharp mum, you know.' Frank's grin showed white, even teeth, and the curly blond hair was attractively messed, as though he had been tangling it with his fingers.

'The Secret Seven could find it out for certain though. Couldn't they?'

'True facts! . . . What's the latest on the Secret Seven, by the way? How's the Good Work getting along? Come on, I can't wait to hear!'

No one else had cared enough to ask. Kate held Frank's arm, as though she couldn't bear to let it go. In a few minutes, he would go rushing in to cuddle Dawn, and give her the present he would most likely have brought for her. But he would give Kate this little bit of time first. For the hundreth time, Kate forgave Frank for being the one to take away her bedroom. She looked up at him, beaming and chatting, and her heart overflowed with love because someone was being interested in *her*.

16

2

Detective work

Kate caught up with Desmond, trudging morosely
to school. 'You know something?' she said, with
devastating directness. 'My mum thinks it was your
dad done that burglary.'

Desmond flinched, and turned away. 'Shut up,
Frog!'

'Was it, though?'

'What d'you say that for? What you wanna say
that for?'

'All right, all right, you don't have to shout at
me. I was only being sym-sym-*sympathetic*!'

'Well don't bother!'

'All right, *be* like that.'

Kate veered to the right, and Desmond veered to
the left. They walked in silence with the width of
the pavement between them, to the end of the road
and round the corner. Kate chewed her hair, con-
sidering the position, and squinted sideways at
Desmond. 'Anyway, it ain't your fault, is it?
Nobody's saying it's your fault.'

Desmond glared at the ground, and kicked at a
broken paving stone.

'I mean it, Desmond,' Kate blundered on.

'Oh, shut up! Shut up! . . . *You* wanna know
something? All right, I'll tell you. My dad's going
straight, he is! He nearly got a job the other day.
See?'

'You mean he didn't do the burglary?'

'Oh, you got it at last. Well done.'

Kate beamed at him. 'There now. Why didn't you say so before?'

In the playground, Desmond merged with a gang of boys who were kicking a ball about, and Kate stood by herself. She watched the clique of girls who called themselves the Super Six, standing in a huddle under the shed. Their arms were tightly linked to keep warm, little puffs of white mist coming from their mouths, and swirling away in the bitter air. They twittered and gasped and said 'Ooh-ooh-ooh!' in tones of enjoyable outrage, every now and again; and Kate felt lonely, and left out.

The Super Six was named after the Secret Seven, in a way, only it wasn't for detecting. The Super Six was for combing your hair in different styles, and for criticizing other people's clothes, and for sharing any bits of scandal that came along. Kate would dearly have liked to belong to the Super Six, but for some reason they didn't seem to want her.

There were only three other girls in Class 7 who weren't in the Super Six. These were Faridah and Nasreen, who usually only spoke to each other – and Suzette, who got bronchitis every winter like Dad, so she was away from school more often than not. Kate hated the days when Suzette didn't come to school.

Mrs Warren always let people sit with their friends, which was fine except when your one friend was away. Kate scuffled sadly into the classroom this morning, and took her place opposite Faridah and Nasreen, with just an empty chair beside her.

The Super Six were all together, of course, gossiping away at the next table. '*Maths!*' said Mrs Warren, warningly.

Kate did not like maths, she much preferred reading. These days there was always one of the Secret Seven books under her table – opened, so she could snatch a quick comforting read every now and again. Percentages today, for instance, was boring and she didn't properly understand it. Kate kept abandoning Percentages to see how the Secret Seven were getting on with a notebook they had found, all in code.

'I need a rubber!' said Natasha. 'Who's got a rubber!' She was a big girl, well developed; she knew a lot of grown-up things that nobody else knew until Natasha told them, and the Super Six had been her idea.

'Quietly, Natasha!' said Mrs Warren. It was one of Mrs Warren's snappy days.

'You can borrow mine,' said Kate.

Sarah was away this morning, as well as Suzette. If Kate lent Natasha her rubber, Natasha might let Kate be in the Super Six just for today, mightn't she? Just to make up the numbers?

'Thanks, Frog!'

'Must you be so rude, Natasha?' said Mrs Warren, who was snappy because she was on a diet, and very, very hungry.

'*I* don't mind,' said Kate. She minded quite a lot really, being called Frog, but she wasn't going to let Natasha see.

'She got bulgy eyes,' said Natasha. 'Just like a frog, look at them!'

'It don't matter,' said Kate, earnestly. 'I don't mind.'

'If you had to wear glasses like Kate,' said Mrs Warren, 'your eyes would look just the same.' Mrs Warren herself had nice eyes, warm and sparkly.

She was making a great effort to become thin and beautiful, so the rest of her would match her eyes. Mrs Warren was continually making herself thin, and letting herself get fat again.

Natasha smirked, and patted her hair, secure in the awareness of her own bold good looks.

'I don't mind, anyway,' said Kate.

The Secret Seven had found a list at the end of the notebook that wasn't in code and that might be a record of stolen goods. Do burglars usually make a list of things they steal, then, Kate thought? How exciting if I could find one! I already found a burglary, so one day I might find a list as well. It would be a clue. I could help the police. She dragged herself away from the story to have another go at Percentages. It wasn't coming right, though – she had made a mistake. 'I need my rubber back!' she whispered, across the tables.

'In a minute,' said Florence, making free with Kate's rubber, uninvited.

Kate waited a minute. 'I want my rubber,' she said, again.

'Patience, patience!' said Natasha.

'You are so impatient, Frog,' said Ranjit.

Kate chewed her mouse-coloured hair, and wrinkled her nose up and down so the glasses nearly fell off. Natasha whispered something to the others, and they all snorted with laughter as though Natasha had said something very witty. They looked at Kate, and nudged each other, and snorted into their books again. Kate got up. 'Give me my rubber!' she said, in a loud voice.

'Give Kate her rubber back,' said Mrs Warren's voice, from somewhere at the back of the class.

Florence threw the rubber, so it struck Kate on

the side of the face. Her cheek stung, but not as much as her hurt feelings. She lunged across the tables and scrubbed indiscriminately with her rubber at Florence's book.

'Stop it, Frog!' Florence was a big black girl, with a dull heavy face. I'm cleverer than Florence, thought Kate. So why did they choose her to be in the Super Six and not me?

'What are you doing, Kate?' It was a pity that Mrs Warren wanted so much to be thin and beautiful, when really she was meant to be fat and jolly.

'Rubbing out Florence's work,' said Kate.

'I beg your pardon!' said Mrs Warren.

'Rubbing out Florence's work.' Surely Mrs Warren had heard her the first time.

'Oh Kate, really, whatever next!'

'That's all,' said Kate. 'There won't be any next. Florence wanted to use my rubber so I helped her. I done it to save her the trouble; she should be pleased.'

'Neither a lender nor a borrower be!' No one quite understood what that meant, though they had heard Mrs Warren say it often enough.

'Kate don't need a rubber anyway,' said Florence, sullenly. 'She ain't doing her work; she's reading. She got a book on her lap.'

'Ha, *ha*! Is that right, Kate?'

'Yes.'

'Give me the book, you can have it back at home time.'

'Oh, Mrs Warren, *please*!'

Mrs Warren held out her hand. Kate sighed. 'I just now come to the exciting part, though. I wonder if the Secret Seven are going to catch the

21

criminals. Do *you* think the Secret Seven are going to catch the criminals, Mrs Warren?'

'Without the least shadow of doubt!' said Mrs Warren, taking the book and putting it into her drawer.

At playtime, little flecks of snow drifted over the yard. The boys screamed and whooped with joy, and begged the skies for more. The Super Six shivered, and stamped their feet, and blew on their fingers. Kate stood as near as she dared, singing a wordless song, and commenting to herself out loud.

'Tra-la-la – I know something nobody else knows . . . Tra-la-la-la – I know something exciting, but nobody else in this class knows it . . . Tra-la, tra-la, tra-la! I'm not going to tell *anybody* my exciting thing.'

'What exciting thing?' said Ranjit.

'Don't encourage her,' said Natasha. 'She's doing it for attention!'

'Tra-la-la,' sang Kate.

'Come on, Frog!' said Jennifer. 'If you got something to say, say it.'

'Don't encourage her!' said Natasha.

'You wanna hear it, then?' said Kate.

'No,' said Natasha.

'All right, I'll tell you,' said Kate. 'I found a burglary. Yesterday. At somebody's house in this school.'

'You mean little Jacob,' said Marie. 'That's not news, Frog, we know all about that. *All* about it,' she added, meaningfully.

'Jacob is my cousin,' said Florence.

'Don't encourage her!' said Ranjit.

By late morning, the snow was falling thick and fast. Dinner-time play was a cramped and unsatisfactory business, indoors because of the weather, the wonderful snow visible through tall classroom windows, but tantalizingly out of reach. Kate longed to get on with the Secret Seven, but the book was still in Mrs Warren's drawer, which was locked, and Mrs Warren was in the Staff Room, making the most of an apple and two small water biscuits. Mrs Warren would not care to be disturbed on one of her diet days.

She came back to class for afternoon school, but now it was time to get the painting things out. Mrs Warren's stomach rumbled dismally, as she scolded the boys. 'Are you *trying* to tip that water pot into Matthew's lap, Ashraf? Do you usually paint with your elbows, Curtis? I saw that, Daniel! Yes, Daniel, you *do* know what I'm talking about . . .' Friday afternoon was a niggly time of the week anyway, and the classroom as usual seemed to be just full of boys.

The Super Six leaned their heads towards each other, and whispered. They were whispering about the boys, probably about the ones they fancied, Kate thought. She considered pretending to fancy someone herself, just to be in it. 'Who likes Curtis better than Daniel?' she said, in a fairly loud voice, inviting discussion.

The Super Six ignored her.

'Who thinks Curtis is good looking? *I* do!'

The Super Six ignored that, also.

Kate dipped her brush into blue paint and painted large rings round her eyes, outside the glasses. 'Look what Frog's doing!' she heard Ranjit say.

She dipped her brush into the black paint and gave herself a magnificent curly moustache, reach-

23

ing halfway up each cheek. Faridah and Nasreen regarded Kate's antics with unsmiling faces, but Ranjit and Jennifer giggled and egged her on. 'Do a beard, now!' said Jennifer.

Kate painted a beard.

'Don't encourage her,' said Natasha; but she was laughing in spite of herself, and so were all the Super Six. Excited by this success, Kate painted her nose in mottled red and purple.

'You silly little clown!' said Mrs Warren, just noticing. Her plump figure had been bent over Desmond's table, but she straightened up now, her curves straining against the tight green jumper, a jumper which had been bought last time Mrs Warren was thin. The boys began to guffaw and cat-call, sprawling over the tables, and falling about with mirth.

'Do you mind!' said Mrs Warren, furiously. 'Look what you're doing, Matthew! You're going to have that paint on the floor in a minute!'

'What a fruit and nut case, though!' said Curtis, grinning all over his handsome black face.

'She's potty!' said Natasha. 'They'll have to put her in the loony place, I think.'

'Yeah!' The Super Six nodded and sniggered, and elbowed one another.

'Leave off being mean to Kate!' That was Desmond. He spoke up suddenly in his gruff voice and everyone looked, because Desmond didn't usually say much in class. Kate.was as surprised as anyone, but her heart warmed with gratitude that someone was standing up for her.

'You shut up, Desmond!' said Natasha. 'We know something about you!'

'That's enough!' said Mrs Warren. 'I won't have

24

any more bickering in this classroom! Kate, go and wash your face.'

Irritability subsided, up to a point, and when Kate came back from the cloakroom everyone was getting on with their work. But presently Curtis sidled up to Natasha and whispered in her ear. Natasha whispered back to Curtis, and Curtis went into a huddle with the other boys on his table. There was hissing, hands shielding mouths, and subdued whistles. There were sidelong glances, and more whispering. Kate watched what the boys were doing, with a troubled face.

On the next table, Desmond sat with closed expression, making purposeless stabs at his painting. He knew they were talking about him. He knew what the talk was about. The rumours in the street had spread to the school, and there was no escape now because the Super Six had got hold of it. Now *everybody* was going to be saying those lies about his dad. Now everybody was going to be looking at *him*, and saying, 'That's the person whose dad was a thief once, so he must be a thief still.'

For ever, and ever, and ever. They would say it for ever and ever. And it wasn't fair!

Home time came, and the snow had stopped falling, but the sky was grey and thick with the promise of more. The playground came joyfully to life, as shouts and flung snow bounced from wall to wall.

A snowball hit Desmond, full in the face. He brushed it off with his sleeve and crunched on, head down, across the spoiled white carpet. 'Come on, Des!' said Daniel.

'Yeah, come on!' said Ashraf.

'I think he's shamed!' said Natasha, scornfully.

25

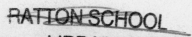

'Come on, Des!' called Matthew. 'Come and play!'

Desmond made a circle in the snow, all the way round Daniel and Ashraf. Daniel threw another snowball – not hard, just a little friendly one. There was nothing personal, Daniel would like to say, in the way the boys had been enjoying the gossip about Desmond's dad; it didn't mean they had anything against *Desmond*.

Desmond trudged on, across the playground and through the gate.

'Leave him!' said Natasha. 'He's shamed because of his dad.'

'It's not true though, what you been saying to each other,' said Kate.

'Shut up, Frog! What d'you know about it?' said Natasha.

'A lot, actually.'

'Come on then, tell us!' said Marie.

'Don't encourage her!' said Natasha. 'She's just making out!'

'You're saying Desmond's dad done that burglary, but he never. He told me.'

'Ha, ha, ha!'

'What do you mean, "*ha, ha, ha,*" saying it like that?'

'You believe everything people tell you, don't you, Frog!' said Natasha.

'But it's true!' Kate insisted. 'Desmond's dad's going straight, now. He is! He nearly got a job the other day, so that proves it!'

'Ha, ha, ha!'

'. . . You're horrible, Natasha!' said Kate, suddenly.

26

'Shut up, Frog. Who do you think you are, talking like that to me?'

'Yeah, said Ranjit. 'Who do you think you are, talking like that to Natasha?'

'I'm *me*, of course,' said Kate. 'And do you know something? I wouldn't be in your Super Six now for a hundred million pounds!'

'You'd be in it for nothing,' said Jennifer, 'if we let you. You'd pay *us* to get in, Frog, so don't make out!'

Kate shook her head. 'Not any more.'

'She's potty,' said Natasha. 'Don't encourage her.'

'I think you *want* it to be Desmond's dad done that burglary, though,' said Kate. 'That's why I think you're horrible. That's why I don't want to be in the Super Six . . . Hooray! Hooray! I don't want to be in the Super Six no more! I just discovered it!'

She twirled her school bag round her head, and went tripping and sliding through the snow, with a strangely light heart. If she hurried, she could catch up Desmond before he reached Wessex Road.

Desmond had a stone today, a large flat one, which he was using to scrape the snow from the tops of boundary walls as he passed. The snow tumbled in powdery cascades, all over Desmond as he walked. He was beginning to look like a snowman.

'Wait for me!' called Kate. She was out of breath, the cold air like knives in her chest, as she gulped it in. 'Wait, Desmond! Wait for me!' Desmond went on trudging, and sweeping the snow off the walls.

Kate walked beside him, and leaned her head to beam at the glowering face, under its hood. 'Hello!'

she said, brightly. Desmond went on trudging, and sweeping the snow off the walls.

'What are you thinking about, Desmond?'

Desmond went on trudging, and sweeping the snow off the walls.

'I bet you're thinking about the horrible things that lot been saying. I bet it's that!'

He snarled at her, then. 'Get lost!'

'Do you know what I think? I think they're a load of silly mad cows!'

'Belt up!'

'Is that what *you* think, Desmond?'

'Leave me alone!'

'No. I won't!'

Desmond began to walk more quickly, and Kate hurried as well. 'Push off, Frog!'

'Don't you want to know my idea I had?'

'Nope.'

'Are you sure you don't want to know it?'

'You heard!'

'All right, I'll tell you . . . . Are you listening?'

'No.'

'Right. It's about the Secret Seven.'

'What's that?'

'*Desmond! Everybody* has heard of the Secret Seven! It's like the Famous Five.'

'Oh, I know now. Some book, innit?'

'Didn't you never read none of them?'

'Can't be bothered with reading books, can I? Reading books is rubbish.'

'But this is a good one! This is a good one, Desmond! It's about some children that make themselves into detectives. You can read the book and see how to do it.'

'Do what?'

'Be a detective!'

'I don't wanna be a detective.'

'Well I do, I do! I want to be a detective to find out who done Jacob's burglary. And all the others.'

Desmond turned his head away.

'Don't *you*?'

'Nah!'

'I bet you do really! I bet you would really like to be a detective, to find out who is doing the burglaries, so everyone will know it's not your dad!'

Desmond swept the snow off someone's wall and sat down. His lips were pulled back, showing one broken front tooth, and Kate flinched from the pain in his face. 'Is it very hard, then?' he said, dragging out the words.

'Is what hard?'

'To be a detective.'

'I don't think so. Anyway, it's not hard for the Secret Seven. The first thing you do, you have to look for clues.'

Desmond stared at her, with eyes that did not appear to see. Then he got off the wall. 'Let's go!'

'You mean home?' said Kate, disappointed.

'Nah! What you said, innit! Look for clues.'

'We'll be the Secret Two then, shall we?'

'Nah!'

'What then?'

'Nothing.'

'We ought to have a name, though.'

'Belt up, Frog! Don't go on about we have to have a name. It's rubbish having a name. If you go on about we have to have a name, I'm going home.'

Kate tossed her head. 'All right, *be* like that!'

'So where do we look, then?'

'In Jacob's house of course, dum-dum!'

'Don't call me dum-dum!'

'Don't call me Frog!'

'Ah . . . come on!'

Jacob's house was behind them now. They retraced their steps and called through the letter-box, like yesterday. 'Jaco-o-b!'

He came to the door, a small lonely figure. 'I'm scared the burglars might come back.'

'Don't worry, they won't,' said Desmond. 'They took all your stuff, already.' Desmond had not read the Secret Seven, but he was wise in the ways of burglars.

'We come to look for clues,' Kate explained.

'The police done that,' said Jacob.

'Well we come to look for some more. We come to look for the ones the police didn't find.'

'What *are* clues, really?' said Jacob.

'I'll explain it,' said Kate. 'What we have to look out for is a notebook, in code. With a list of stolen things on the back page. Well anyway, something like that. Most likely it will be out the back. In the garden.'

'Will our telly be on the list?' said Jacob.

'Most likely.'

'Why would they make a list, though?' said Desmond. 'What would they stop to make a list for?'

'I dunno, but it's in the book.'

'It must be a rubbish book,' said Desmond. 'I'm going home!'

'Go on, then.'

'. . . Yeah . . . Well . . . After we had a bit of a look, I suppose.'

'Can I be in it?' said Jacob.

'Of course,' said Kate. 'We can be the Secret Three.'

'Shut up, Frog!' said Desmond.

They searched a long time, digging about under the snow, but there was no notebook in the tiny back garden, nor in the front one either. 'Can we see if they dropped it inside?' said Kate.

They poked hopefully into corners, and Kate opened a few drawers. 'Don't do that,' said Desmond, uneasily.

'How can I find the notebook, though, if I don't look?'

'I don't think there *is* any notebook.'

'Perhaps the burglars didn't drop it this time,' said Kate, unwilling to admit this might be so.

'I'm going home,' said Desmond.

'What about in the bedrooms?' Kate wondered.

'You can't go looking in people's bedrooms, they don't like it!'

'Your mum won't mind, will she, Jacob?' said Kate. 'Your mum will be pleased, that we're going to catch the burglar for her.'

'Yeah,' said Jacob, entering into the spirit of it.

The drawers in the bedroom had been ransacked by yesterday's visitors, and their contents stuffed back any old how by Jacob's mother. Kate stirred the mess up some more. 'Let's leave it, now,' said Desmond.

'Why?'

'Jacob's mum's going to come.'

'So? Don't matter! Stop moaning.'

Kate left the drawers, and tried to crawl under the bed, but there was not enough space for that so she lay on the floor and groped with her arms. 'I think I found it!'

What she had found was an old pair of winter boots, with something stuff into one toe. 'It's paper, anyway,' said Kate, excitedly. 'It must be something!' The paper crackled as she pulled it. 'Oh!' Her face fell. 'It's not a notebook after all.'

'What, then?'

'Just a load of money.'

'That's right,' said Jacob. 'That's my mum's secret hiding place. The burglars never see it, yesterday.'

'Not much of a villain didn't find that!' said Desmond, scornfully. 'My dad would have found it. That *proves* it's not my dad.'

'I can hear my mum,' said Jacob. There was the piping of very young voices as well.

'You never shut these drawers, Kate!' said Desmond, doing it quickly, before Jacob's mum should come and find them open.

Next moment, there was a banging and a shrieking, and fury in the room. 'What you lot think you're doing in here? What you . . . ? I don't believe it . . . you little thieves! Get out of my bedroom now! Get out, get out, before I fetch the police here again!'

'Oh we aren't *thieves*,' said Kate with a reassuring smile. 'And Jacob said you wouldn't mind.'

The two little ones, just collected from their child minder, began to cry. They were tired and hungry, and there had been too much shouting and distress already in this house, since yesterday. 'Stop that, Chantal, before I get my hand to you! Nadine, I'm warning you! Jacob, you're going to get a good beating for this! Oh yes, you are, no use looking at me with them cow eyes!'

'You don't understand,' said Kate.

'Yes I do, I understand all right! I know what's going on, I wasn't born yesterday! I know who *you* are!' she said to Desmond. 'You're that Locke boy, ain't you? I know what you was doing in them drawers, you was looking for something to steal. Get out! I don't want none of *your* family in this house!'

'But I told you,' said Kate. 'We *aren't* thieves. Actually we're detectives.'

'Pull the other one, it's got bells on!'

'Don't you say nothing against my family!' said Desmond, tears of rage in his eyes.

'I'll say what I like about your family! And *you*, Kate whatsyourname! What's your mother going to say? What's your mother going to say when she finds out who you been going about with, leading you into bad ways?'

'Desmond is a very good person to go about with!' said Kate, indignantly. 'And he never thiefed nothing in his life, I don't think. And if you mean about his dad's been in prison, his dad's going straight, now, so that's all you know!'

'Huh! That's why the police got their eye on him for all these break-ins, I suppose.'

'He's got a alibi!' Desmond shouted at her.

'Oh yeah, I'm sure!' said Jacob's mother. 'He's sure to have one of those! . . . Out! Out! And don't come back!'

'Don't you worry about that unkind person, Desmond,' said Kate, pushing him down the path. Outside it was dark already. The street lights were on, but thick grey clouds wrapped the unfriendly street in a blanket of cold, and discouragement.

'I hate her!' said Desmond.

33

'Let's forget her!' said Kate. 'Let's go on looking for clues, eh?'

Desmond said nothing. He stood by the gatepost and trembled.

'Eh, Desmond?'

Desmond picked up his stone, and began pounding it on the gatepost of Jacob's house, his face working.

Kate kicked around in the snow at her feet, her eyes intently on the ground. Nothing. She moved down the road, still churning up the snow in case there might, by some miraculous chance, be something important underneath.

Ah, what was this? Kate bent and picked it up. Not a notebook, but a piece of paper, certainly. A piece of paper with writing on it! The paper was wet from the snow, and the pencil writing faint; Kate stood under a street light and squinted at the words through her crooked glasses.

'It's a list!' she called excitedly to Desmond. 'It could be the one, you know! It could be!' She peered closer at the paper. 'It says *telly*!' she squealed. 'Desmond! It says *telly*!'

That proved it, of course! Jacob's telly had been stolen, the word *telly* was on this paper – what else could the paper be but the burglar's list? Dropped in haste yesterday, as he fled from the scene of his crime. Excitement cleaved its way upwards, slicing through Kate's chest; excitement so sharp that it hurt. With shining eyes she turned to call at Desmond once more.

She was just in time to see him heave his stone through the front window of Jacob's house.

3

Police!

Desmond's legs churned into sudden action. He stumbled past Kate, still paralysed with dismay under the street light. He came back for her, and dragged her along the snowy pavement – fast at first, then casually; they could have been any two children sauntering home from school, albeit very late.

'What did you do that for, though, Desmond?' said Kate.

'Do what?'

'Throw that stone.'

'What stone? I never throw no stone!'

'Yes you did, I saw you!'

'No you never, you never see nothing! If anybody ask, you never see nothing. Got it?'

'. . . Oh.'

Shouts were coming from far away; there was crying, and hysterical screams ringing faintly down the street. 'Do you think it hit somebody?' said Kate, deeply troubled.

'What? What hit somebody?'

'The stone.'

'What stone?'

'The one you – All right, forget it!'

'We went straight home, remember?' said Desmond. 'After we come out of Jacob's house we went straight home.'

'All right.' She understood how hurt and angry

he was, of course. Anybody could understand that. But what he did was going too far, wasn't it? Surely that was going too far!

'They can't prove nothing,' said Desmond.

'Can't they?'

'Only if you tell!'

'All right, then, I won't.'

She didn't feel all right, though, she felt terrible. The stone had gone crashing through that window with the frightening sound of broken glass. Suppose Jacob had been in the room, or one of his little sisters? Suppose the stone had hit one of them on the head? Or a piece of glass had gone into their eye? Kate would have liked to run back, really, and find out what happened, only she couldn't do that because she wasn't supposed to know anything about it, was she?

The house reeked of paint. Behind the closed sitting room door were the usual sounds of Dad coughing and the telly blaring. 'Fra-a-a-ank!' called Dawn's thin high voice, above the other sounds.

Frank was in the kitchen, standing on a step-ladder. 'Fra-a-nk!' came Dawn's voice, again. Frank winked at Kate, and cupped a hand over his ear, pretending he couldn't hear properly.

'Like to get this finished before your mum comes home,' he said, sloshing away at the shabby walls. He was painting them buttercup yellow. The coat underneath, what was left of it after Frank's rubbing down, was so old it was difficult to say *what* colour it was meant to be.

'It's a surprise,' said Frank. He seemed very excited about it. 'How you think your mum's going to like my surprise?'

This was a hard question to answer, since you

never knew which way Mum was going to go. '*I* like it, anyway,' Kate declared. She watched Frank for a bit, and in the safety and ordinariness of home, her worries began to fade. A thought occurred to her. 'Didn't you go to work today, Frank?'

'There wasn't none,' said Frank.

'No *work*?'

'Recession, innit! Be something next week, perhaps.'

Frank was on something called 'price work'. This meant that if nobody wanted any painting and decorating done just now, Frank had no work and no money. This was worrying, with the baby coming and furniture for the new home to save for. 'Ain't you worried?' said Kate.

'Nah, not really. Something'll turn up. Where you been, anyway? I thought school finished half past three.'

Dawn and Dad, watching television in the sitting room, would not even have noticed. 'I've been detecting,' Kate told Frank. That bit was all right to say, wasn't it? She wasn't used to hiding things. There had never been anything of importance to hide, before.

'Like the Secret Seven?'

'Yes. Actually, *I'm* in a gang now. It's called the Secret Three.'

'Goody, goody, gumdrops! Can I join?'

'*Really*? Do you want to?' Kate's cheeks had gone pink with pleasure.

'Sure. Got any clues yet, then?'

'*Yes*,' said Kate, suddenly remembering the piece of paper still clutched in her hand. 'I think it's a list of the things the burglars took from Jacob's

37

house.' She peered at the paper, through her crooked glasses. 'Oh!'

'What's the matter?'

'It says "telly", but the rest is all vegetables. Carrot, and potatoes and stuff.'

'Probably a code,' said Frank.

'Oh, *yeah*!' Kate beamed her gratitude at Frank for reminding her. The picture of that stone, going through Jacob's window, was fading rapidly now. It raced away into the dark parts of her mind, like a bad dream that you start to forget as soon as you wake.

'Give it to me,' said Frank, reaching down from the step-ladder. 'I'm good at breaking codes.'

'*Are* you?' said Kate, admiringly.

Frank sat on the ladder and studied the piece of paper hard. 'I think . . . Wait a minute, wait a minute . . . No . . . Yes . . . *Got* it!'

'What!' said Kate, jumping up and down with excitement. 'What does it say?'

'Well now, *you* think it says "carrots, potatoes, lemons",' said Frank. 'But what it *really* says is "gold, diamonds, money"!'

'Does it? Oh, but the burglars didn't find the money in Jacob's house!'

'Didn't they?'

'No. The money was hid in a old boot, under the bed. Jacob's mum always puts her money there.'

'Good for her!'

'So why is it on the list?' said Kate, puzzled.

'Perhaps I made a mistake,' Frank giggled. 'Perhaps it says "carrots, potatoes, lemons" after all.'

'If you're only going to tease, you can't be in it!' Kate reproached him.

'Sorry. All right, I'll be serious. No, I will, I will, on my mum's life!'

'It's not a code really, is it?' said Kate, disappointed.

'You never know! . . . Let's have a crack at it, and see.'

'How?'

'Well – try different letters, innit? Like, C could really be A. And A could really be T. You have to have a pencil and paper, and keep trying till you get it right.'

'I don't understand.'

Frank came down from the ladder, wiping the paint from his hands. 'I'll show you. Just a minute while I pack this lot up. Have to finish it tomorrow after all. Can't let down the Secret Three!'

'Mum's coming now, anyway. You can show her the surprise.'

'Blimey!' said Mum, throwing open the kitchen door, and fanning the air with her hand. 'What a stink!'

'It's a surprise,' said Kate.

'Well thanks very much I'm sure, but how am I supposed to get the tea?'

'Take-aways tonight,' said Frank. 'My treat.'

'You can't afford it!' Mum protested, not very hard.

'Who says?' said Frank.

Dad coughed, and retched as though his insides were coming up. Mum opened the sitting room door. 'It's the fumes!' he spluttered.

'Oh, stop moaning!' said Mum. 'And make room for the breadwinner on that sofa. Gawd! I think it's my turn to have the bronchitis or whatever. Nice bit of 'flu going around, I think I'll have that next week . . . Trouble is, I reckon this family would fall apart if I done any such thing!'

'I can't help it if I keep getting these pains,' said Dawn.

In the kitchen, standing up because there was no room for even a stool, Kate and Frank worked at the burglar's list. 'This is how you do it,' Frank explained. 'You got CARROTS, POTATOES, LEMONS, PARNSIPS, SOAP. Now, take the letter you got the most of, and change that first.'

'It's A,' said Kate. 'No — S!'

'So change that. Say S is really T. Now see what you got.'

Kate wrote out the list again. CARROTT, POT-ATOET, LEMONT, PARTNIPT, TOAP. 'It doesn't make any sense at all, now.'

'Course it doesn't. You got to change all the other letters now. Say A is really O. Now what have you got?'

Kate wrote them. CORROTT, POTOTOET, LEMONT, PORTNIPT, TOOP. 'It's going to take a long time to get it right,' she said, doubtfully.

'True facts!'

'Suppose we change all the letters, and it still doesn't make any sense?'

'Then we got to start all over again and make every letter something else.'

'Isn't there a quicker way?'

'Why don't you have another read of the Secret Seven, and find out?'

'Oh, *yes*!'

'I'll go up the chippie and get the take-aways while you're doing it.'

'All right.' Now he had given her the idea, Kate couldn't wait.

40

She found the book and read it standing up, running her finger along the lines. 'Oh, *no*!' she exclaimed suddenly. She read the page again, to make sure, then slammed the book shut. 'It's a cheat! It's a cheat! It's not fair, the lady that wrote this story! She didn't ought to make it such a cheat!'

Kate felt hurt and betrayed. For the moment, she had gone right off the Secret Seven. That notebook in the story, the one the children had found – that notebook hadn't been dropped by the burglars at all! That notebook had been planted, as a trick, by someone's horrid little sister. It wasn't a real clue, it didn't mean anything!

Sadly, Kate regarded the piece of paper she had just now been labouring over so earnestly. Now she really came to look at it, she saw quite clearly that the first word wasn't TELLY at all, it was JELLY. What she had found was nothing more important than someone's shopping list!

Oh well, good job she hadn't wasted any more time on working it out! Good job about that.

There was a sharp knocking at the front door. Frank back with the take-aways? Frank forgot to take his keys? Kate flew to the door to let Frank in.

On the doorstep stood a young policeman. 'Are you Kate?' said the policeman, smiling at her.

Out of the dark parts of her mind, the picture of Desmond throwing his stone flashed back. The picture was bright, and clear, and terrifying. Kate gulped, and swallowed her panic. 'I don't know nothing about it,' she assured the policeman.

'Oh?' said the policeman, still smiling. 'You don't know nothing about what?'

'Nothing!' said Kate, wildly. 'I don't know nothing about nothing!'

'Who is it at the door?' called Mum, from the sitting room.

'It's the police,' said Kate.

She felt quite funny, standing in the cold hall, waiting with dread for whatever was going to come next. Her knees were weak, she found; and her head seemed to be floating, not properly joined to the rest of her. She chewed hard on a piece of hair, for comfort.

Mum came out, her eyes hard and suspicious. 'What's up, then?'

'Are you—?' The policeman consulted his notebook. 'Are you Mrs Jackson?'

'Yes. Who wants to know?'

'Do you mind if I have a little talk with Kate, here?'

'Well, not on the doorstep . . . That's right, bring in half the Arctic with you! I love clearing up after people, it's my favourite occupation . . . . No, sonny, I didn't say open the perishing door *again*. I got a sick husband in there, you know!'

'Sorry,' said the policeman, meekly. 'Do you mind, then, if I have a word with Kate?'

'What's she been up to?'

'Nothing, I hope. Just thought she might help us clear up a little mystery.'

'What is it?' called Dawn from the sitting room, above the noise of the television.

'Nothing much!' called Mum. She glared at the policeman, implying that it had better *be* nothing much, or Mum would not be pleased.

'I don't know nothing about it,' Kate's voice sounded quite faint.

'So you said,' said the policeman. 'You don't

42

know nothing about nothing. But I think you must have heard something, Kate, at least.'

'Heard something when?' said Mum.

'What is it?' Dawn stood in the doorway. If anything interesting was going on, she didn't want to miss it.

'Someone threw a stone,' said the policeman, 'through the front window of Number 6. Late this afternoon. Kate had only just left the house when it happened, we do know that.'

'What was you doing in Number 6?' Mum barked at her. 'You supposed to come straight home from school, what was you doing going in Number 6?'

'Ooooh, *Kate*!' said Dawn.

'Did anybody get hurt?' Kate's voice was so shaky now, it had almost disappeared.

'You answer me!' said Mum.

'Luckily, no,' said the policeman.

'I was only detecting,' said Kate. 'About the burglary.' Relief and apprehension were chasing round inside her now. Round and round, and faster and faster. Like a spinning top. Like a bicycle wheel. Kate tried to grab at the spokes of the bicycle wheel in her head, to make the thoughts slow down.

'And when you finished your detecting?' said the policeman. 'What happened then?'

'Nothing. We come home.'

'We?'

'Me and Desmond.'

'Now we're getting somewhere!' said Mum.

'I never see Desmond throw no stone,' said Kate, earnestly. 'I never!'

'Did you *hear* it?' said the policeman.

'I never hear nothing.'

'I think you must have, Kate.'

43

Kate's teeth chomped away at the piece of hair. 'Well?'

'I might have heard *something*,' Kate conceded. 'Yeah, I remember now, I did.' She began nodding vehemently, up and down. 'Yeah, I did. I heard all glass breaking.'

'And where was Desmond, when you heard that?'

'He was walking beside of me.'

'Did you say anything to each other, about the breaking glass?'

'Course we did. I said "somebody's throwed a stone through the window." And he said, "Oh yeah, somebody's been and throwed a stone." . . . Or something like that.'

'Actually,' said the policeman, 'your chum says what you said at first. He says he heard nothing!'

'Well, he would, wouldn't he!' said Mum, butting in unexpectedly. 'Poor little blighter! Scared to death he was going to get accused, wasn't he!'

'Do *you* think Kate's telling the truth, though?' said the policeman.

'Telling the truth? Of course she's telling the truth! Don't you try saying my daughter's a liar! My daughter's not a liar! We don't tell lies in this house. Only sometimes . . . I hope you're listening to me!'

'She seems to have changed her mind once or twice this evening, though.'

'Well, that's you, innit! Mixing her up! . . . And that other poor kid! . . . It's blimming disgusting. It's blimming disgusting the way everybody got their knife into that family. Anything goes wrong it must be one of them Lockes done it.' Yesterday Mum's voice had been raised as loud as anyone's against Desmond's family; but that, of course, was yesterday. Today, Fate had put the Jacksons and the Lockes on the same side.

'He ain't a bad kid, you know, that Desmond.' Mum rattled on. 'He ain't a bad kid at all, really. He just ain't going to have a chance, is he, with people bad-mouthing him all the time!'

'He hasn't actually been accused of anything,' said the policeman, cautiously and not quite truthfully. Jacob's mother had been loud and bitter and definite, that Desmond was the one who threw the stone. Unfortunately, she hadn't actually seen him do it. No one had actually seen him do it. Or at least, no one was prepared to say.

'Is that all, then?' said Mum.

'Well—' said the policeman.

'That's all then, is it?' said Mum. She advanced, and the policeman backed. It ought to have been the other way round really; but the policeman was very young, and Mum was very fierce.

She would have opened the door and ushered the policeman out, only just at that moment the door opened anyway, and Frank stumped into the hall. 'It's like the North Pole out there!' he declared. The cheerful smile froze on his face when he saw the policeman. 'Blimey! The Law!'

'He come about Kate,' said Dawn, with some relish.

'Shut up, you!' said Mum.

The policeman opened his mouth to have one more go at Kate, but Frank butted in, his eyes swivelling theatrically heavenward. 'All right, the game's up! I done it!'

'Done what?' said the policeman. He was not at all satisfied with Kate's answers, and not at all

45

proud of himself for being intimidated by Mum. And now there was this clown, trying to be funny.

'IT. Whatever you come about. I confess.'

He's doing it to save me, Kate thought gratefully.

'Leave off your nonsense!' said Mum, grinning.

'It's all right, I'll go quietly.' Frank pranced in front of the policeman, his wrists extended. 'Aren't you going to put the handcuffs on, then?'

Mum screeched with laughter. 'A right comic, ain't he?' she said. 'Has us all in stitches, sometimes.'

'Stop messing about, Frank!' said Dawn, crossly.

'What's the matter with you, face-ache?' said Mum. 'He's not doing no harm. He cheers the place up. Lot more than can be said for some!'

Frank grinned at Dawn. He didn't mind her crossness, he found it quite endearing. Indeed, Frank was charmed by almost everything Dawn said, or did. She was the miracle in his life. She was wonderful.

'I know you from somewhere!' said the policeman, suddenly.

'You do?' said Frank.

'Hillesden High?' said the policeman.

Frank clapped the policeman suddenly, and delightedly, on the back. 'Stuart Sunderland!'

'Frank Hodges!'

'Well, what do you know!'

'Long time no see!'

'True facts!'

'Well, what do you know!'

'What do you know!'

'What do you *know*!'

'Are you going on saying that for ever?' said Dawn, pouting.

Frank giggled, and put his arm round her to take the jealous look off her face. 'Stuart and me's old mates. We was at school together. Hillesden High.'

'I wouldn't never have guessed!'

'Ever see anything of the old gang?' said P.C. Sunderland.

'Nah! Not for years.'

'Me neither . . . . They were good days though, weren't they? The things we got up to!'

'What things?' said Dawn.

'Oh, we were real bad lads!' said the policeman, laughing.

'Were you?'

'Nah . . . just larking. Some of 'em were a bit over the top, though . . . . Remember Spotty Dick, Frank?'

'Who's Spotted Dick?' said Dawn.

'A right character! Wonder what happened to him?'

Frank shrugged. 'Who knows? Anyway, I got other things to think about now,' he said, with pride, indicating Dawn.

'Some blokes got all the luck!' said the policeman, eyeing Dawn appreciatively. She was looking particularly attractive today, wearing the more becoming of her two maternity dresses, the one with the rainbow stripes. Round her neck was the locket on a chain which Frank had brought for her last week; a cheap little present, but pretty and it suited the dress.

'Come on, you!' said Mum, pushing Kate into the kitchen. 'I don't think we're needed at the old boys' reunion. Here, give me these,' she said to Frank, coming back for the parcel of fish and chips

47

he had brought. 'We're just going to have our tea,' she said, pointedly, to P.C. Sunderland.

'See you around, then,' said P.C. Sunderland, uncomfortably, to Frank.

'Not if I can help it!' declared Dawn, as the front door closed.

'He's all right,' said Frank. 'What's wrong with him, then?'

'I don't like him. He was a bad lad, he said so!'

Frank hugged her, and hugged her. What she really meant was she didn't want Frank to have any friends except her.

'And I got this nasty pain . . . .'

'Have you?' said Frank, anxiously. 'Shall I go out and phone the doctor?'

'Oh, it's not bad enough for the *doctor*.'

'Let's have a sit down and a cuddle,' said Frank, leading Dawn tenderly into the sitting room.

'Everybody keeps opening the door!' Dad complained. 'What did that policeman want?'

'Oh, forget it!' said Dawn, her face muffled against Frank's chest. 'What you want to go on about that for?'

'Old Duffy won't like the police coming for us,' said Dad, anxiously.

'Don't worry,' said Frank. 'Worry makes you old.'

'Dad always thinks we're going to get throwed out,' said Dawn.

'Who by?' said Frank. 'The Invisible Man?'

They giggled together, snuggling close.

In the kitchen, Kate chewed her hair and trembled with apprehension. Frank and Mum between them had saved her from the policeman, but there was still Mum to be faced.

'All right, don't tell me!' said Mum.

'Don't tell you what?' said Kate, twisting her nose with the lopsided glasses, so she could squint sideways at Mum.

'Don't tell me nothing! I don't want to know!'

'Oh,' said Kate. 'Can I have a biscuit?'

'You'll spoil your tea.'

Kate munched one anyway. 'Can we have a dog?' she said, pushing her luck.

'No,' said Mum. 'We can't have a dog.'

'It would be good, though. It would bark, and keep the burglars away.'

'We don't need a barking dog. We got your dad.'

Kate giggled. She was recovering rapidly from her fright. It had been fairly horrible, but the horribleness was over now. A worry-free evening stretched ahead.

After the meal Kate fetched *Good Work Secret Seven* once more, and sat in a corner of the sitting room to read it. She sat on the floor, her fingers firmly in her ears because the television was very loud. Dawn's arms were firmly clamped round Frank, in the armchair. Dad coughed. Mum did the ironing while she watched, and interrupted every programme to laugh, or jeer, or argue with the person on the box. It was a fairly typical evening.

Kate read, with a mounting sense of excitement. Of course, of course! The first clues were always wrong ones; she had forgotten that, hadn't she – or more likely she had never properly understood it. She understood it now, though, she understood it now! First the wrong clues, and then the right ones. The Secret Seven had found a spectacle case and a button. The spectacle case was another wrong clue, but the button was going to be a right one, she was sure, she just knew it!

Well – that could be just like her, couldn't it! That could be just like Kate. She had found the silly list; she had been through all that. And now she knew about the spectacle case she could miss that bit out and go straight on to the button. Or it might not be a button exactly, but anyway something of the sort. Something that came off the burglar's clothes.

Only where was she going to find this clue? She couldn't go back to Jacob's house to look for it, not now. What was really needed, of course, was like in the book. What was needed was for the thief to steal someone's car, like in the book, and leave his button in the car, like in the book. Then she and Desmond and Jacob could find it, like in the book, and go on being the Secret Three.

Or the Secret Four, if Frank was going to be in it, only it looked like Dawn wasn't going to let him, now. What a pity Dawn had to spoil things so much.

Anyway, the problem was – whose car could the burglars steal? Nobody in *her* family had a car. And nobody in Desmond's family had a car. And nobody in Jacob's family had a car. It was a nuisance, but there it was. There was only one thing for it – there would have to be another burglary. There would have to be another burglary, so the Secret Three, or the Secret Two, or the Secret One or whatever, could find the clue and solve the mystery, like in the book.

There were no burglaries all weekend. Kate went up and down the road on Sunday, in what was left of the snow, but there was no sign of a break-in anywhere. She hid behind a tree for some time, thinking perhaps the burglars would come if they thought no one was looking, but still nothing happened. Only Bruce, being exercised up the road, greeted her ecstatically, jumping up and down and wagging his whole hindquarters. Kate cuddled Bruce, and when Mrs Harris asked her what she was doing all by herself behind a tree on a cold winter's day, Kate said, 'Nothing.' Mrs Harris had already stolen one of Kate's burglaries, she wasn't giving her the chance to steal another, no way!

Kate wandered round the block, and round the next block, and round the next block again. She thought of calling for Jacob, but the sight of the broken window, temporarily patched with cardboard, rather put her off that idea. She thought of calling for Desmond, but she had never been to his house, and wasn't even sure of the number.

Kate also realised that she didn't really want to see Desmond, today. She didn't really want to see him tomorrow, either. He might want to talk about the policeman coming, and she didn't want to. He might want to know about the questions, and what she said, and what the policeman said, and she didn't want to talk about it. It was over, it was finished with. She didn't want to talk about it any more, and she didn't want to remember it.

There was one thing she couldn't quite forget, though. She couldn't quite forget that Desmond was a dangerous person, who threw stones, when you weren't expecting him to, through people's front windows! You could get to be a bit frightened of a person like that.

4

A disastrous mistake

The snow was almost gone. Just a few crusty patches lingered on the pavement, dirty and depressing in the bleakness of Monday morning. Kate saw Desmond ahead of her, scuffing at the snow patches with his down-at-heel trainers, and she slowed her own steps so as to keep a good distance between them. At the corner she stopped, and counted quite deliberately to a hundred. That should make Desmond out of sight before she turned into the next street.

In school, the Super Six were fussing round Marie, whose birthday had been yesterday. Marie was eleven now, and to prove it she had brought her cards and presents for the others to admire. One of her presents was a very attractive bracelet. Kate craned her head across the tables, so she also could see the bracelet that everyone was admiring so much. It was certainly very unusual; the links were wide blocks of some dark transparent substance, with clusters of tiny gold-coloured pins and half moons set inside. 'It's *old*,' Marie said proudly. 'My uncle bought it for me in the market.'

'Couldn't he afford a new one, then?' said Kate.

'That's all you know, Frog!' said Natasha. 'Old things are *better* than new things. Old things are more valuable.'

'My uncle said there probably isn't another

52

bracelet like this in all the world,' said Marie, quite
bursting with pride.

'Get on with your work, girls!' snapped Mrs
Warren. Mrs Warren was much disgruntled about
the disappointing news her bathroom scales had
given her that morning. She had wriggled and wriggled, trying to make the needle go down a bit
further, but the needle had refused to oblige. And
she hadn't cheated on her diet once. Not all the
weekend! Mrs Warren looked for some outlet for
her disappointment, and her eye fell on Marie's
bracelet, at that moment on Natasha's wrist.

'Ha, ha! What's that I see you wearing, Natasha?'

'Nothing,' said Natasha, putting her arm under
the table so Mrs Warren couldn't see the bracelet.

'You know you're not allowed to bring jewellery
to school!' said Mrs Warren.

'*I* didn't bring it to school,' said Natasha, virtuously.

'Well now you can give it to me,' Mrs Warren
gloated. 'I'll look after it till home time.'

'Look what you done now, Frog!' Natasha
accused her.

Marie was privately quite relieved that Mrs
Warren had taken the bracelet away. She had been
getting a bit worried that Natasha was going to ask
to keep it – it was not very easy saying no to Natasha. But Marie pretended to be angry with Kate,
so she could keep in with the others. 'If you hadn't
have been too nosy, Mrs Warren wouldn't have
seen!' she hissed.

'Tra-la-la!' sang Kate, to show she didn't care.

And she had less reason than ever to care, this
morning, because, hooray, hooray, Suzette was
back! There she sat, in the seat next to Kate, wear-

53

ing two jumpers one on top of the other to protect her delicate chest. The pasty face was blank, the watery-blue eyes without spark – but she was *there*. Kate beamed and beamed, because Suzette had come back to school.

'Get on with your work, everyone!' said Mrs Warren, bored with their squabbles already. And it was only Monday morning!

'I know something about Kate,' said Florence suddenly, out loud.

'What?' said Natasha.

'More work, less talk!' Mrs Warren thought she must say that out loud in her sleep, sometimes.

Florence whispered to Natasha.

'You wanna hear this, Mrs Warren!' said Natasha.

'No I don't,' said Mrs Warren. 'Not unless it's very important.'

'It is!' said Natasha. 'Kate Jackson threw a stone through Jacob's window, on Friday.'

'Oh, you liar! I never!' Kate was outraged at the false accusation, and besides, it was over, it was finished with! What did people want to start bringing all that up again for?

'That ain't what I said, Natasha,' said Florence. 'I never said Kate done it, I said Desmond done it probably, but Kate was there.'

'Ha, ha!' said Mrs Warren. 'Can this be true, Kate?'

'No!' said Kate, going very red, though.

'Desmond?'

'No. What d'you think?' Desmond's face was sullen, his voice tight, and hoarse. It *was* true, of course, but they had no right to say it. They couldn't prove it, so they had no right to say it.

Desmond sat in his place not looking at Mrs Warren, not looking at anyone.

'See!' said Kate. She tossed her head at the Super Six, then found a nice comforting piece of hair to chew.

'What do you know about it *actually*, Florence?' said Mrs Warren.

'Jacob is my cousin. He tell me yesterday.' Behind her hand, Florence poked her tongue out at Kate. 'See!'

Kate took the piece of hair out of her mouth. 'It's nothing to do with me anyway,' she said, defiantly. 'Or Desmond!' She put the piece of hair, all wet and stringy, back into her mouth.

'Oh well, I suppose it's outside school,' said Mrs Warren, suddenly losing interest.

'*See!*' said Kate, taking the hair out of her mouth once more, so she could poke her tongue back at Florence.

At playtime, Kate wrapped her arm round Suzette's neck and dragged her into a corner, well away from the Super Six. 'Guess what?' she said.

'I dunno.'

'No, but guess, guess!'

Suzette considered. 'Something to eat?'

Kate's arm gave Suzette a little shake. 'Something *exciting*!'

Suzette considered again. 'I can't think of anything exciting.'

'I'll give you a clue,' said Kate. 'It's to do with the Secret Seven. *Now* can you guess what it is?' She beamed at Suzette to encourage her, but Suzette's face remained blank, the mouth slack and half open.

'Give up?'

Suzette nodded.

'You and me are going to be detectives!'

The exciting news did not actually seem to excite Suzette very much. 'How's that, then?'

'We're going to be the Secret Two. Or it might be the Secret Three if Jacob still wants to be in it. Desmond was in it first, but I think it's better without him, really. Just you and me, eh? What do you think?'

'I don't mind,' said Suzette.

'Aren't you going to ask what we have to do?'

'Yeah, all right, what do we have to do?'

'We have to find a burglary, and look for clues.'

'All right, then.'

'We'll look after school then, shall we?'

'All right, then.'

Out of the corner of her eye, Kate saw that the Super Six had joined forces with Curtis and the boys. Their heads were all together, and they kept looking at Desmond, who was skulking by himself. Curtis and Matthew seemed very amused about something, and Kate was afraid she knew what it was. Why couldn't they let it alone? Why couldn't everybody just leave it alone, and let it get forgotten?

Daniel and Ashraf were dissociating themselves from the others. They had withdrawn from the sniggering group, and now they were circling Desmond, enticing him to a game. Desmond kicked at the ground and wouldn't look at them. Daniel had a kind heart and hated to see people unhappy; he went right up to Desmond and leaned an arm on his shoulder.

'Get off me!' Roughly, Desmond shrugged off

Daniel's arm, and slouched against the playground wall, his expression hard and bitter.

'Come on, Des!' wheedled Ashraf.

'No. You say bad things about me!'

Daniel and Ashraf gave up.

After play there was a programme to be watched in the television room, and Curtis managed to wangle a place next to some boys from another group, so he could spread the gossip a bit further. Desmond lurked at the back of the room, and wouldn't come near the rest of the class. 'What's the matter, Desmond?' said Mrs Warren.

'They're saying bad things about him,' said Matthew.

'And you!' said Ranjit. 'You're saying the bad things as well!'

'Yeah – well. . . .'

'It's all true, anyway,' said Natasha.

'You take that back!' said Desmond.

'It's true!' said Natasha spitefully. 'It's true, it's true, it's true!'

'If you don't stop stirring it, Natasha, you're going to be a very sorry young lady,' Mrs Warren warned. 'Now. All eyes this way!'

Mrs Warren turned to switch on the television, and Natasha turned to mouth 'True', once more, at Desmond.

Desmond charged. He charged head down at Natasha, knocking over a few chairs, and two or three other people, to get at her. Nasreen and Faridah screamed, Desmond's fists flailed at Natasha, and Natasha, who was actually quite a bit taller, pounded the back of Desmond's neck and kneed him frantically in the stomach.

The expression on Desmond's face, what could

be seen of it, was murderous; no one dared to interfere . . . except for Mrs Warren, who had once attended judo classes. The judo classes had gone the way of the Italian classes, and the Russian classes, and the classes for flower arranging, but had at least left Mrs Warren conveniently equipped for separating fighting children.

'Now shake hands! Go on, I said shake hands! . . . Hurry up, or the programme will be half over before we get to see any of it! . . . I'm waiting, Natasha. I'm waiting, Desmond! . . . The television is not going on till you two have made your peace with each other. . . . Right, that's it! Back to class, everyone!'

There was a chorus of protest.

'QUIETLY!' said Mrs Warren.

They jostled to form an unwilling line by the door. 'It's not fair!' 'It's Desmond's fault!' 'It's all your fault, Desmond!' 'It's all your fault we have to miss our programme!'

'It's true about the stone, as well,' said Florence, just loud enough to be heard.

Desmond went berserk. He rampaged through the rows of chairs, now fortunately empty, kicking some over, and hurling others about. Faridah and Nasreen screamed again.

A few grim strides, and Mrs Warren had Desmond in her grip. 'All right. All right. All right, Desmond!' He was a morose child, always – hard to get through to. But he wasn't a loner. He mixed reasonably well, in his uncommunicative way, accepted by the others in spite of his surliness. And he had never been known to be violent, not counting the odd scuffle in the playground. He must be very upset about something, to start behaving like this.

Mrs Warren hugged Desmond, reassuringly. 'All right,' she soothed him. 'It's all right!' He trembled in her grasp, but he was calm now. 'Shall we talk about it somewhere private?' Desmond shook his head, his face dark with misery. If Mrs Warren's empty tummy had not just then clamoured so piteously for attention, she might have coaxed him further. As it was, she only said, with diminished interest: 'Pick the chairs up then, and we'll all get back to class.'

'Isn't he going to have a punishment for that?' said Natasha, indignantly. She felt sore in lots of places from where Desmond had been punching her. She was sure she was going to have lots of lovely bruises to declaim over, as soon as she had time to look for them. 'He should be suspended or something.'

'When I need your advice I'll ask for it, Natasha,' snapped Mrs Warren.

Kate was horrified. She chewed a piece of hair, and squinted at Desmond sideways. He hadn't actually thrown the chairs *at* anyone, but he could have hit someone by accident, all the same. He could have hit Mrs Warren when she went to cuddle him. How brave of Mrs Warren to cuddle Desmond, when he was doing those terrible things!

'I don't think I like Desmond any more,' she said to Suzette. 'We won't have him in our detecting for definite! Eh?'

'All right,' said Suzette.

'It started off to be *for* Desmond, really. To prove it's not his dad that's the burglar. But it doesn't *have* to be for that. It can just be for us, for fun.'

'All right, then,' said Suzette.

Kate would have liked to tell Suzette about

Desmond and the stone. With all this fuss she had started to worry about it again, and it would have been a relief to be able to share the worry. But she had promised not to tell, so she wouldn't. She wouldn't be friends with Desmond any more, but she wouldn't tell on him. Not to anyone, not ever.

And now she really must try to forget all these unpleasant things! *Good Work Secret Seven* was nearly finished, and, by good fortune, in the afternoon was Free Choice. Kate threw herself into the last chapters of the book, so that once more the shadows around her receded, and only the story shone bright and real.

And it was true what she thought, it was true! The button *was* a real clue! She was right all the time, she was right; now all that remained to do was to put what she knew into practice!

At home time, Suzette prepared to go straight home. 'What about our detecting?' said Kate.

'What detecting's that?'

'*You* know!'

'Oh.' She had forgotten. 'I have to go home, though. My mum said I must go straight home.'

Out of the corner of her eye, Kate was aware of Desmond lurking by the school gate – all by himself, watching her out of hooded eyes. He's waiting for me, she thought, in something like a panic. She seized Suzette's arm, and pressed close to her friend for protection. '*Suzette*! You said you would be the Secret Two, with me!'

'I have to go home, though.'

'Well I'll come with you! We'll do the detecting in your road, how about that? On the way to your house.'

'All right. . . . I don't mind.'

Kate steered Suzette through the school gate, and safely past Desmond. 'Hey!' he called in his gruff voice. 'Where you going, then?'

'I think Desmond wants to talk to you,' said Suzette.

'No, he doesn't. Come on, we have to find a burglary.'

'All right, then.'

Desmond glared with hurt eyes at the retreating backs of the two girls. He had been looking forward to walking home with Kate, he'd been really looking forward to it. He'd been *counting* on it. He'd had an idea over the weekend, an important idea about this detecting thing. And since it was Kate's idea that had got him thinking in the first place, it made sense to put their two ideas together, didn't it?

Only now, for some reason he didn't understand, Kate wouldn't talk to him. What was the matter with her? Why was she being like that?

The others were all against him, but he did think *Kate* was on his side. He really thought that, when she wanted to help him clear his dad's name, and she didn't tell on him, about that stone! When she didn't tell on him about the stone today, he thought Kate Jackson was the best person in Class 7, probably – and now she wouldn't even speak to him.

They were all against him now. The whole world was against him.

Choking on bitterness, Desmond began to make his lonely way home. Anyway, he comforted himself, I got away with it about that stone, didn't I! The police couldn't make me admit it, could they? That policeman tried, but he couldn't make me! And it must be he couldn't make Kate neither, otherwise he would have come back.

Why won't Kate talk to me now?

All right, if Kate won't talk to me I'll do my detecting by myself. I don't *need* anybody else, I'll do it all by myself.

Walking in the opposite direction, Kate chattered happily at Suzette. 'We have to find a button or something, that the burglar dropped, and that will be a clue.'

'All right, then.'

'We can start looking now. We can look in all the roads, on the way to your house.'

'All right, then.'

The streets were dull and peaceful, all the houses cosy-looking and undisturbed. 'These burglars are getting very lazy!' Kate complained.

'I wonder what's for tea,' said Suzette, with more animation than she had shown all day.

'Look!' said Kate, in sudden excitement.

'Look what?'

'There!'

'Where?'

'*There* of course. *There*! That van thingy!'

'It's just a van.'

'But that man! Look what he's doing!'

Suzette gave the man her careful attention. 'He's putting a telly in the van,' she concluded.

'But he might be stealing it! He might be the burglar!'

'Shall we tell the police?'

'Well, not *yet*. We have to find the button first.'

'All right. . . . Why do we have to find the button, though?'

'It's in the book.'

'Where is it, then? This button?'

'I don't know, do I? It could be anywhere.'

'Shall we look tomorrow? I have to go in my house, now.'

'Oh, not yet! Not yet, Suzette! Let's look round the van. Quick! Before he drives away.'

The girls ran towards the parked van, which was facing them. Kate was not in the least bit frightened. No one in the Secret Seven ever got hurt, so what was there to be frightened of? In any case, the driver was only a shadowy, unreal figure, safely shut away inside the van.

The van's engine was running noisily, but the driver and his mate seemed in no hurry to move. The driver sat sideways in his seat, smoking a cigarette and leaning over something on the seat beside him. Suzette began to cough. Somewhere in the glow of Kate's excitement was a small dark patch of guilt, like an ink stain. She had made Suzette run, and hurt her chest. She couldn't stop now, though, not now! She dragged Suzette to the back of the van. 'Get down!' she whispered. 'So he can't see us!'

Suzette was coughing too much to answer. The patch of guilt inside Kate darkened, and spread. She peered under the van. There was a squashed up coke tin, and something else!

In the blaze of rapture which followed, the patch of guilt vanished. 'I think that's it!' Kate breathed. 'I think it's the button!'

Suzette had stopped coughing. She crouched against the van, out of sight of the driver, taking deep breaths. She had only the vaguest idea what she was doing there. What was it all about? She was Kate's friend at school, and that was good. They played skipping together in the playground,

63

and were each other's partner for P.E. and outings. These things were reasonable, and easy to understand. But all of a sudden it seemed they had to be detectives. They had to look for burglars, and buttons, and really Suzette would much rather just keep to the skipping, and the safe feeling of knowing you were always going to have somebody for your partner. She watched Kate scrabbling under the van, and wished she could go home for her tea.

Kate stood on the edge of the kerb, with the object in her hand, gazing at it in wonder and triumph. Hooray, hooray! *Now* the book was coming true! True, it was not actually a button, but a buckle that might have come off someone's belt. Never mind, though – the buckle was near enough. She pushed it into her school bag, and discovered she was not at all sure about what to do next. What was the button supposed to be *for*, exactly? . . . Oh yes – you had to match the button with the criminal's clothes. . . . But how were you supposed to get near enough to him to do that? Confused now, and uncertain, Kate felt for her glasses, which were hanging from one ear, and almost falling off her face.

And at that moment, something quite terrible happened.

Suddenly, without warning, the van reversed! Not very fast, and not very far, but enough to send Suzette flying. She landed with a thump, on her side; was silent with shock for a moment, then began a series of such lusty shrieks and wails. It seemed very unlikely that she could have been seriously hurt. Suzette always made a fuss like that, when she bumped herself.

The van shot forward, stopped with a jerk, and

the driver leapt out. He was big and burly, with a large florid face and his hair in a pony tail. He was also shouting some very bad words indeed, and Kate was suddenly terrified of him. He was no longer unreal, no longer safely shut away in the van. He was out in the street, and coming after her, and he was *bad*.

Kate ran.

This bit wasn't supposed to happen at all, it wasn't in the book. What had gone wrong? Oh, what had gone wrong? Kate ran full pelt to the end of the road, and round the corner, and round the next corner. She didn't dare stop. There were footsteps pounding behind her, but she was scared for her life to turn round. Bad people had knives! Bad people did terrible things to little girls!

The footsteps came nearer, and nearer. Kate pushed herself to run faster, and her knees began to sag. Her breath was coming in great gasps that stabbed at her chest, and she couldn't run any more. Helplessly, with a sick dread in her heart, Kate's legs folded up, and she collapsed in a crumpled heap on the pavement.

And the footsteps caught up with her, went round her and past her. . . . There was a muttered 'Out the way, kid!' and she saw him go. With incredulous eyes, Kate watched him disappearing down the road – a lanky black youth, on some pressing mission of his own, nothing to do with her whatsoever!

Now Kate became aware of other people in the road. Not many. People didn't come out of their houses for fun, on raw January afternoons. But there was a woman with a shopping basket, and another with a baby in a pram. Both were watching

Kate from the opposite pavement, wondering if she was ill perhaps, and if they should offer assistance.

And now on the same side as Kate, coming towards her, were Natasha and some of the Super Six, accompanied by an assortment of younger brothers and sisters belonging to Ranjit and Florence.

'Do you see what I see?' said Marie.

'What's she sitting in the road for?' said Florence.

'Having a nice rest, Frog?' called Ranjit, grinning.

'She's potty!' said Natasha. 'She does it for attention. Don't encourage her!' She fingered the unusual bracelet on her wrist as she spoke, holding it up to admire the gold-coloured pins and half-moons. Natasha was a great deal more interested in Marie's antique bracelet than she was in Kate.

Kate began to cry. The others reached her, and halted to investigate.

'What's the matter, Frog?' said Marie, in a kinder tone.

'The b-burglar!' Kate sobbed.

'What's she on about?' said Florence.

'She's potty,' said Natasha. 'Don't encourage her.'

'She got burglars on the brain,' said Ranjit. 'Her brain is gone mouldy, because of all the burglars in it.'

'Like mouldy cheese,' said Florence.

'That's all *you* know, then!' said Kate, recovering a bit. 'There *was* a burglar! I see him take the telly, so there!'

'Mouldy cheese,' said Florence, again.

'What telly?' said Marie.

66

'Out of a house. In – what's it called now? Where Suzette lives. Bossington Drive.'

'She's making it up,' said Natasha. 'She's doing it for attention.'

The younger brothers and sisters, having no interest in this conversation, pulled and whined. Suddenly Kate began to cry again, loudly and in earnest. '*Suzette*!. . . . I think the burglar has got her!'

'Really, though?' said Marie. 'Do you really think that?'

'All right,' said Natasha. 'Let's go and see.'

'Suppose they got a gun or something?' Ranjit was doubtful about taking chances.

'Frog probably imagined it all,' said Natasha. 'Out of her loony head. But we'll go and see, just in case.'

Kate trailed at the back of the group, chewing a piece of hair. The patch of guilt had reappeared. It spread, and spread, swallowing fear, filling her mind with thick, dark, suffocating remorse. She had run away! She had left Suzette, and only thought about herself, and run away! Of course the burglar had caught Suzette! Suzette couldn't run, she had a bad chest. Besides, besides. . . .

No, Kate wouldn't think about besides! She wouldn't, she wouldn't! Suzette was only a little bit hurt, she must be! She *had* to be only a little bit hurt, because anything else would be too terrible, and it wasn't in the book! It wasn't in the book to get caught by burglars either, though. . . . Kate struggled, as she followed, to make sense of it all.

Round the corner, and into Bossington Drive. 'Right!' said Natasha. 'Where is this burglar, then?'

The van had disappeared. Suzette had disappeared also. 'The van was just here,' said Kate. 'Behind that yellow car, I remember!'

'Well, it's not here now,' said Ranjit, on the whole relieved.

'So where's Suzette?' Kate was distraught; her worst fears were coming true.

'Perhaps the burglar took her,' said Florence, with some relish.

'Oh, yeah,' said Ranjit. 'In the van!'

'Did you get the number of the van, Frog?' Natasha was beginning to be interested. Not *too* much interested, of course. That would make her look silly, later on, if the whole thing turned out to be a false alarm.

'No,' Kate admitted.

'Why ever not?'

'I don't know. I didn't think of it. It wasn't in the book.'

Natasha snorted her scorn.

'Perhaps Suzette ran away,' said Marie, 'like you did, Frog. Most likely she ran home!'

Kate shook her head. 'She couldn't run.'

'Why not?'

'It makes her cough to run. And anyway. . . .'

'Anyway, what?'

'She got knocked down by the van!' Kate's words came out in a rush of anguish.

'*What!*'

'She got knocked down by the van. . . . I don't know what happened after that.'

'Perhaps she's dead,' said Florence, cheerfully.

Kate began to cry again, great heartrending sobs. 'I think we should go to Suzette's house,' said Marie.

'And tell her mum?' said Florence. 'That she might be dead?'

'Get real, Florence!' said Natasha.

'She might just be in hospital,' said Marie.

'Long as the burglar didn't take her,' said Ranjit. 'You know – in the van.'

'We should go to her house anyway,' said Marie. 'And find out!'

'I was just going to say the same thing,' said Natasha.

They hung about, in the tiny front area, while Natasha rang the bell. A tearful woman came to the door. 'Is Suzette in?' said Natasha.

'Who wants to know?'

'We were just wondering,' said Natasha.

'Is that Kate Jackson?' said the tearful woman. 'Hiding behind that gatepost?'

'It was nothing to do with *me*,' said Natasha.

'I don't know how you got the nerve to show your face round here, Kate Jackson!' called the tearful woman. 'Properly upset me, you have! A real nasty shock you give me!'

'Is Suzette all right?' said Marie.

'Just about, no thanks to Miss Marple here! . . . A real nasty shock she give me!'

Florence giggled.

'You think it's funny, do you! Suzette's been sick, you know! First day back at school, and something like this got to happen! She's a bag of nerves, you ought to see her. She won't be out tomorrow, that's for certain.'

'Did he let her go, then?' said Ranjit.

'Did who let her go?'

'The burglar. The one in the van.'

'Oh yeah, the burglar! We mustn't forget the burglar! . . . Was you all in it then?'

'Not me,' said Natasha.

'If you want to know, it was your "burglar" brung her home!' said Suzette's mother. 'Only he wasn't actually a burglar. He was just a bloke collecting a telly from up the road. Which the owners *asked* to be collected! To be mended. Because there was somethink gone wrong with it. . . . Satisfied?'

'I thought that's what it was,' said Natasha. 'I thought all the time, it was that. Didn't I say, Marie, I thought they must be taking the telly for repair? I said that, didn't I, Ranjit! All the time.'

Kate wished for a deep hole to appear, in the pavement, so that she could jump into it. She squinted sideways at Natasha and Ranjit, and saw the gathering malice on their faces. She dreaded the next day in school. Next day in school was going to be horrible, she just knew it!

5

Desmond has a plan

'Found any good burglaries lately, Frog?' said Natasha, with a cruel little smirk.

Kate looked the other way, leaning on her elbow, and chewing a piece of hair. She was not easily embarrassed, but she did feel dreadfully embarrassed today.

'How's the burglars getting along then?' Kate could feel Florence's horrible grin, scorching its way through the back of her head.

'Work!' said Mrs Warren.

'Did you know Kate is a detective, Mrs Warren?' said Natasha. 'She thinks she's Miss Marple.'

'Ha, *ha*!' said Mrs Warren.

'Yeah. She's brilliant, actually. She detected the telly man, yesterday. Wasn't that clever!'

'I suppose you never make mistakes, Natasha.'

'Oh yeah, I do make mistakes. I made a mistake to think Kate Jackson is not absolutely bananas, only she is!'

'That will do.'

'All right, Mrs Warren. I thought you might like to know why Suzette didn't come to school again today, that's all. I was just trying to be helpful.'

'You've lost me. Am I supposed to see some connection?'

'Suzette got knocked down by the telly van!' said Ranjit, savouring every word.

'What!'

71

'Yeah!' said Florence. 'She could have been killed, couldn't she!'

'And it was all Kate Jackson's fault,' said Ranjit.

'I think you'd better tell me about it, Kate,' said Mrs Warren.

Kate's cheeks burned.

'Come on, spit it out! I haven't got all day.'

'I was only looking for the button.'

Florence gave a loud snigger.

'Something amusing you, Florence?' said Mrs Warren, tartly. 'There's something amusing, about people getting knocked down, in the street? Come on Kate, let's have the rest of it!'

'It was the lady that wrote the book's fault, not mine!' Kate burst out. 'She said about the button, that come off the burglar's coat, and I was looking for it.'

The whole class was listening now, wide grins on nearly every face. 'Kate's got a gang called the Secret Three,' said Florence, suddenly remembering that bit, gleaned from her cousin on Sunday.

Light began to dawn. 'You mean like the Secret Seven?' said Mrs Warren. 'But that's a *story*, you little goose! You aren't supposed to *believe* it!'

The class rocked with merriment. Faridah and Nasreen did not laugh, of course, because they hardly ever did. And Desmond did not laugh; Desmond watched, with sullen angry eyes, raging inside himself. They didn't ought to pick on Kate like that! He would like to punch them, all of them in the class that were doing it. He remembered Kate wasn't speaking to him, and he still didn't know what that was about, but it didn't make any difference anyway – he would still like to punch the ones that were picking on her.

72

Kate was silent. Deeply shamed, she chewed frantically at her piece of hair.

'All right you horrible lot, that's enough!' Mrs Warren was sorry now about calling Kate a goose. 'At least Kate *reads*, and that's more than can be said for some of you. And I daresay plenty of successful burglars have got away with pretending to be the telly man, so that bit wasn't so silly. . . . But playing round a parked van – now that's something else, isn't it, Kate!'

Kate nodded, miserably.

'AND HOW MANY TIMES—?'

'I won't do it again,' Kate whispered.

'How badly is Suzette hurt?' said Mrs Warren.

'Not much,' Natasha conceded. 'I think she was mostly frightened.'

'Good! Frightened out of her socks, let's hope!' And Mrs Warren went back to the business of trying not to think about food.

At playtime, most of Class Seven collected in a knot, getting the details from the Super Six. Faridah and Nasreen were not in the knot, of course, and neither was Desmond. Faridah and Nasreen were with some girls from the third year, and no one knew, or bothered, where Desmond was. The rest were having a high old time at Kate's expense, hooting and whistling and falling about with derision. Presently some of the boys broke away, to surround Kate where she stood alone. 'You got a gang, then?' said Curtis, with a mocking grin.

'No,' said Kate. 'Not now.'

'Can I be in it?'

'There isn't nothing left to be in.'

'Can *I* be in it?' said Ashraf. 'Can we be the

73

Secret Four? No, the Fantastic Four – that's more better!'

'What about the Fantastic Five? No – the Filthy Five! How about that?'

'That's a good one!'

'Ha, ha, ha!'

'The Soppy Six! Can we be the Soppy Six?'

'Shut up, Curtis, you going to have Natasha after you, she heard you say that!'

'Oooh, Curtis! *Natasha!*'

'Shut up, you!'

'How about the Silly Seven?'

'The Seven Sausages!'

'Ha, ha, ha!'

'The Eight Extra-Terrestrials!'

'Oh, leave me, leave me!' said Kate. The teasing was too much. Kate stamped her foot, and the tears welled.

'Oooh, she's getting her temper up!'

'You got a temper then, Frog?'

Kate ran into the girls' toilets, and stayed there.

When it was time for dinner play, she went to the toilets again, and shut herself in. No one came to look for her, anyway. Perhaps the joke had gone stale. Perhaps the class had forgotten all about it.

At home time, Kate discovered that they had not.

The boys started it up while everyone was getting their coats. 'How about the Nutty Nine?'

'Nutty *One*, you mean!'

'Don't be so rude about Miss Marple,' said Ranjit. 'This is Miss Marple, you know. This is Miss Marple, everybody, the important lady detective!'

Kate struggled into her coat, and fastened the buttons with trembling fingers. There was a lump in her throat, and a funny sort of churning in her stomach. What she wanted to do was run down the stairs, and across the playground, and home; home where nobody knew, because she very carefully hadn't told them, the shaming mistake she made yesterday.

Only she didn't think she would be able to do that, because these people weren't going to let her!

In the playground, a crowd of boys taunted Kate. Previously, Kate had taken little account of the boys. Except for Desmond, they had been just a collection of loud and clumsy male things, filling the classroom. Now, suddenly they were a menace – a powerful combined force, ranged against her. And they were big, some of them! And they had strong arms, and rough voices! Kate cowered away from them.

'Come on, Miss Marple!' said Curtis, grinning. 'Coming to catch some burglars?'

'Leave me!'

'Oh, come *on*!'

'Please let me go home.'

'Home? You ain't going home, are you? We ain't going home, are we boys! We're coming with you, to catch some burglars!'

Kate charged at the ring of jeering faces and, miraculously, it parted to let her through. She began to run, but Curtis dodged neatly in front of her. She tried to dodge round him, but found him still in her path. 'Come on then, Miss Marple!' he teased her. 'Get past me! See if you can get past me!'

Kate writhed, and ducked, but Curtis was always there. Behind her, she was aware of cat-calls, and harsh laughter. Nobody was on her side, nobody!

Kate stood still, trembling. Out of the corner of her eye she saw some of the Super Six, emerging into the playground with their various small charges. She saw Desmond as well, watching from afar. Everyone was watching, while Curtis tormented her; in this crowded playground, Kate was frighteningly alone.

Desperately, she made another bid for freedom, but once again Curtis barred her way. His handsome black face leered down at her – to Kate at that moment, a hideous face, a monster face. 'Want any help, Curtis?' called Natasha.

Suddenly, Desmond moved. His short thick body pounded its way across the playground and pulled up sharply, at a metre's distance from Curtis. 'Leave Kate alone!' he growled.

Curtis sniggered. 'Did you say something?'

'You heard!'

'You going to make me, then?'

'Might do.'

'All right, come on! Come on, tough guy, make me!' Curtis was laughing. Desmond was smaller than he was, with no reputation as a fighter, in spite of yesterday's outburst.

Desmond launched himself at Curtis. There were many scores to settle; Desmond settled them with bitterness and fury. And behind the joy of the settling was the thought – she'll have to talk to me *now*, she'll just have to!

Curtis was not prepared for the sort of attack he was getting from Desmond. He himself was feeling playful, not aggressive – he couldn't switch moods at a moment's notice. Before he knew what was happening, and to his great astonishment, he found himself on the ground, with Desmond sitting astride raining blows all over his face. The attention of the crowd switched to the fight. Kate was not interesting any more.

She ran. She ran hard, until she was sure none of them were following her, and then more slowly. Finally she walked, because she was out of breath and there was a stitch in her side, and she didn't feel like running any more anyway. She felt flat, and a bit dead inside. She was safe, but the brightness had gone out of the world. There didn't seem to be anything much left to look forward to.

She heard her name being called, from a distance, and turned to see who was calling. Desmond! Kate began to walk quickly again, because she didn't want to see Desmond. She still didn't want to talk to Desmond, she didn't want to have anything to do with him. The fight was one thing. The fight was a brave rescue, and perfectly proper. But Desmond was also a dangerous person who threw stones through people's front windows; and used his strong arms for beating people up in a *classroom*; and for throwing the chairs about in school.

Desmond called her name again. 'Kate! Kate Jackson! Come on – wait for me!'

Kate stopped. She didn't want to talk to Desmond, but really she supposed she ought to say thank you. It was only manners to say thank you to someone when they saved you from being bullied. She waited, not turning round, while Desmond caught up.

He halted a little way off, and called once more. 'You all right, then?'

'Yeah!' said Kate, still not turning round.

'I give him a lesson, you know. That Curtis. I give him a good lesson.'

'All right.'

'He won't do it again.'

'All right, then. . . . Thank you.' She made herself turn round then, because it didn't seem to be very good manners saying thank you to someone with your back to them.

'Not while I'm around, anyway. He won't do it again while I'm around.'

'Yeah, you said. . . . Thank you.'

Desmond came a few steps nearer. He looked warily at Kate for a moment, then away. She was talking to him anyway, she *was* talking. He found the confidence to say the next bit, the deeply personal bit, the bit he had worked out this morning, while the class was teasing Kate. 'You know what I think?'

'What's that?'

He kicked at the kerb, his head still turned. 'I think you want somebody to look after you!'

'Do you?'

'Yes, I do.'

'Why's that, then?'

'You're going to get in trouble, else.'

'Look who's talking!' said Kate, before she could stop herself.

'Yeah – well. . . .'

They began to walk in silence, not quite side by side, the width of the pavement between them.

'Anyway,' said Desmond presently, 'I think you do.'

'Do what?'

'What I said. Need somebody to look after you.'

Another long silence. '. . . Can't I look after myself, then?'

'Not really. You trust people too much.'

'Do I?'

'Yes, you do. Like for instance, the story that lady writ. You trust that book, and you didn't ought to.'

'I know.'

'So you need somebody to look after you.'

'Like who?'

Desmond began to execute a lopsided hopping walk, one foot in the gutter and the other on the kerb. 'Who do you think?'

'*You*?'

He picked an empty beer can out of the gutter and hurled it ahead of him. His eyes followed the beer can.

'Do you mean *you*, Desmond?' said Kate, again.

'You got it!'

Kate squinted sideways at Desmond. This was such a staggeringly unlikely idea, Kate didn't know how to respond at all. She chewed a piece of hair while she thought about it.

'Can I trust *you*, then?'

'Yeah, you can!'

'Oh. . . . How are you going to look after me, though, Desmond?'

'Well – you know!'

'No, I don't. You tell me.'

'Well – when you want to do some detecting—'

'I *don't* want to do any detecting!' said Kate, fiercely. 'I don't never want to do no more detecting never! Not never in my life! I finished with detecting. I finished with the Secret Seven as well.'

'All right, then.'

He sounded crestfallen, disappointed. Kate squinted at him sideways, again. There was a great loneliness in his face. 'It was only because—'

'All right, all right, I said all right, didn't I!'

'No, but listen, Desmond. I don't think I'm any good at detecting, really.'

'You had the idea of it, though. It was a good idea. And you made me think of *my* idea, it was all because of you.'

'Was it?'

'Yes, it was.'

There was silence again. Deep inside Kate a little warm spark danced, and multiplied, and urged. 'Desmond—'

'What?' His face was turned from her, his eyes on the opposite pavement now.

'If you really want to. . . .'

'No, it's O.K.'

'No, but if you *want* to. . . .'

'Are you deaf or something? I said it's O.K.'

They were in Wessex Road; they were nearly at Kate's house; there was a deep silence between them. But now the little dancing spark had become a glow, and the glow was in every part of Kate. The warmth of the glow cut her off from the silence; she hugged herself, inside the wonderful warmth.

'It's just that I had this idea,' said Desmond, dragging the words out.

'What idea was that?' She saw him through a rosy mist, and the bad things he did went spinning and spinning into the distance.

'It's not out of a book. It's out of real.'

'What is?'

He looked at her, from under hooded lids. 'I was going to do it by myself, but I think it's, like, better with somebody else.'

'What is?'

'Come with me, and I'll show you.'

Kate hesitated, juggling with her feelings. She *had* gone off detecting – hadn't she? . . . But Desmond thought it was a good idea, he said! And she *had* been afraid of Desmond, a bit. . . . But now he wanted to look after her. Someone was actually interested in her enough to want to look after her! She turned to Desmond, beaming. 'Where we going, then?'

He wouldn't do those bad things any more, would he? Probably. He *wouldn't* do them, she just decided it.

Without speaking, Desmond began striding back the way they had come, his arm stretched backwards, beckoning to her from behind. Kate followed.

They turned a corner. Not the one they usually turned on the way to school, but across Wessex Road and into Devonshire Road. At the bottom of Devonshire Road was Somerset Gardens, and here Desmond stopped. 'See that man, looking over his gate?'

'That one?' said Kate, pointing.

Desmond grabbed for her wrist, but at the sudden movement of his arm, Kate cowered away, falling back a step. She hadn't meant to do that. It was just that all her feelings hadn't caught up with each other yet. 'All right,' said Desmond. 'I won't bite!'

'I know.'

'I don't bite, you know! I'm not a cannibal.' Suddenly light dawned. Was *that* what it was about? Was *that* why she wouldn't speak to him before? Was she *scared* of him then, for being rough? Embarrassed, and ashamed, he looked away. 'Anyway, don't point,' he muttered. 'We don't want him to think we're looking at him!'

'I see.'

'Just walk down like normal, pretend you don't notice, and see what he does.'

'All right.'

Kate was nervous, not knowing what to expect. She chewed a piece of hair, and squinted sideways at the man in his front garden as they passed. 'Did you see?' said Desmond, as they reached the end of the longish road and turned yet another corner.

'No.'

'You *didn't* see?'

'No. He just looked at me, I think. I didn't see him do nothing else.'

'Well that was it!'

'Was it?'

'That's what he does. He does it all the time. He watches people.'

'Does he?'

'Yeah, he does. He's always standing there. I seen him lots of times. Every time I go that way I see him. And he watches people.'

Kate was puzzled. 'Lot of people stand in their fronts and watch.'

'In the *winter*? When it's *cold*?'

'. . . Oh, yeah!'

Desmond turned his head, and began kicking at someone's wall. 'That's how they do it, see?'

'Do what?'

'What you think?'

'*I* don't know . . . See where the people go?'

'See where they *come from*!'

Kate was still mystified.

'See where they *come from*. . . . Don't you get it?'

Kate shook her head.

'See what house they come from,' said Desmond,

his head still turned, torn between shame and eagerness. 'See what house is going to be empty. *Now* do you get it?'

'Oh!'

'You *do* get it!'

Kate beamed, delighted to have grasped the point. 'You mean, burglars watch which house is going to be empty so they can go and burglar it! How do you know that, Desmond?'

Desmond shrugged, his eyes on the ground, the pain in his face hidden. 'How do you *think* I know? . . . All right, don't say it, you don't have to say it! . . . What about my idea, then, what about that?'

Kate considered. 'It's a good idea, Desmond,' she said, to please him. 'It's a great idea. There is just something, though.'

'What's that?'

'This is not our road.'

'So?'

'The burglaries was in our road. How can he watch the people in our road when he's standing here? I don't think he's got a telescope.'

'I didn't say he had! There's other ways to know if a house is empty. This is how he does it in *this* road.'

'I see.' Kate's eyes began to gleam, as enthusiasm came surging back. The exciting adventures weren't over yet, they weren't over, they were going to happen after all. 'You're a good detective Desmond!' said Kate, beaming at him. 'You're a *super* detective. You're a super, *super*—'

'All right, it's no big deal! I just happened to think of it. About that man, that's always standing there.'

'So what do we do now?'

'Well – watch him, I suppose. See if he goes to do any more burglaries.'

'We can't see him from here.'

'I know. We'll have to find a spying place.'

Kate peeped round the corner into Somerset Gardens. The man they had passed was still at his gate, and this time Kate got a good look at him. He was white, and about Frank's age, and scruffy looking. He had not shaved today, or yesterday by the look of it. Kate could not actually see the eyes in the head that turned this way and that, but she was sure they were shifty. 'He does look like a burglar,' she said enthusiastically to Desmond. 'Shall we get in that For Sale house, across the road?'

'There's three For Sale houses.'

'I mean the one with no curtains at the windows. The one that's empty already. So nobody won't come out and shoo us away. And good, because that house got a high wall in front. We can keep down there, and he won't see us.'

'Might as well, then. Wait till he's looking the other way.'

At the far end of Somerset Gardens, two women came out of a house and got into a car. Sure enough, the man at the gate followed them with his eyes. The car did not want to start – the dismal growling of a flat battery grumbled down the road. The man at the gate watched keenly, while the women ran the car battery flatter, and flatter. Kate and Desmond sprinted for cover of the wall. The women in the car gave up and went indoors again.

At that point the man at the gate also gave up and went into his house.

'Now what?' said Kate.

'Let's wait a bit longer,' said Desmond. 'He might come out again.'

But it was cold, crouching behind the wall, and their bent legs grew stiffer and stiffer. 'I don't think nothing's going to happen,' said Kate, disappointed. 'I wish those ladies would have started their car. That man might have burglared their house, then, and we could have seen.'

'Shall we try again tomorrow?'

'Yeah, we can, but—'

'I know. It's cold sitting here,' said Desmond. 'You rather not bother, innit!'

'No, it's not that, it's not that! It's just I was thinking – suppose he does the burglary when we're in school anyway!'

'Yeah, right. I was thinking the same thing.'

'So we shall miss it.'

'Yeah, I know. . . .' Desmond seemed about to say something else, then changed his mind and shifted his position instead.

'Anyway, I don't think nothing's going to happen today.'

'Look!' said Desmond, suddenly.

Three young men, one white, two black, were strolling down the road. They were laughing, in a coarse sort of way, and pushing one another about. Kate's head bobbed above the wall to get a better view, and Desmond dragged her down. This time, when his hand moved swiftly to grab her, Kate did not even twitch. 'I didn't jump that time, did I?' she said proudly.

Desmond shrugged. 'All right, all right, you didn't jump. Big deal! See those blokes, though? I know that black one! My dad showed him to me last week. My dad said, "Oh, *he's* out!" '

'Out?'

'*You* know!'

'Oh! . . . Perhaps he's the burglar!'

'Could be.'

'Not the man at the gate after all? . . . Shall we follow this one then, instead?'

'Look!' said Desmond.

Right outside the house the children were watching, the group of young men had stopped. Two of them hung around the gate, the third swung up the short front path and began hammering on the door. 'Is that the one that's out?' said Kate.

'That's him!' said Desmond.

'The one your dad knows? Is he your dad's friend?'

'No way!' said Desmond. 'My dad wouldn't have nothing to do with *his* sort! My dad says he's bad news. . . . Look, here's old Scruffy coming to the door!'

'Looks like the one that's bad news is Scruffy's friend,' said Kate.

There was more laughing, and pushing, and back slapping, then all four young men disappeared inside the house.

'*Well*!' said Kate.

'Get *that*!' said Desmond.

Kate was overjoyed. 'It must be a gang! You know, for burglaring!'

'Yeah – could be.'

'So we follow them, and catch them at it!'

'Yeah. . . . The only thing is . . . I think it could be dangerous. Those ones can get nasty – know what I mean?'

'Don't matter,' said Kate.

There was the uncomfortable memory of herself running away in panic from the telly man; Kate pushed the memory away. Forget that, forget it! That was just practice, that didn't count! And she hadn't had Desmond to look after her then, had she?

'You still want to do it?'

'Yeah, I do.'

'You sure?'

'Course I'm sure. I got you to look after me now, haven't I?' Kate said, with shining eyes.

'Yeah, right! . . . You want to follow them, then, when they come out?'

'I do want to.'

'Even if it's dangerous?'

'Long as we catch them, that's the main thing.'

They waited expectantly, but once again nothing happened.

'They're probably planning it for tomorrow,' said Desmond. 'They probably sussed it out already, what house is going to be empty, and they're going to do it tomorrow.'

Kate was deeply disappointed. 'Why not today?'

Desmond shook his head. 'It's getting to be too late. People coming home from work now. I think they're going to do it tomorrow.'

'Oh. . . . Desmond?'

'What?'

'Suppose we miss it, like we said before, when we're in school?'

'I know. That is the problem.'

'I wish it was Saturday tomorrow.'

'Yeah, I know. Then we could come and watch

all day. We could watch where Scruffy goes, and where he meets the others, and everything.'

'It will be too late if we wait till Saturday.'

'I know. . . .' He punched the wall a few times with his fist. 'Are you thinking what I'm thinking?'

'I dunno. What are you thinking?'

'Are you thinking we could bunk off?'

'No!' said Kate, scandalized. 'I wasn't thinking no such thing!'

Desmond stood up painfully and rubbed his cramped legs. 'I only thought you *might* have been.'

Kate stood up too, and held on to the wall for support, while the pins and needles came into her feet. 'I never bunked school, never,' she explained.

'All right,' said Desmond. 'Forget it.'

Kate chewed a piece of hair and squinted at Desmond sideways. 'My mum would go mad.'

'She's no need to find out. . . . Anyway, I said forget it!'

Kate chewed more fiercely at the hair. 'Do you want me to, then? Bunk school with you, tomorrow?'

Desmond shrugged. 'It's up to you.'

On legs still stiff from the crouching, Kate walked slowly homewards. Desmond trailed behind her, kicking at walls, and pursing his lips in a whistle which wouldn't come. At her own gate, Kate turned to face him.

'Do you really think they're going to do a burglary tomorrow?'

'Yep.'

'It would be exciting to bunk off and follow them, wouldn't it!'

'Yep.'

'If I'm going to do it,' she said, 'I'll put a sign

88

in my front window. So you can see when you pass by the road.' She was proud of that idea – it was just like the Secret Seven. No, *not* like the Secret Seven! Like *her*, like *Kate Jackson*! With enthusiasm, she developed the idea. 'I'll hitch up the net curtain like it happened by accident. And I'll meet you round Somerset Gardens at nine o'clock.'

'You don't *have* to. . . .'

'I know I don't have to. And I don't know if I will, yet, so don't count on it. I will have to have a good think, in the night.'

6

Truants!

Dawn was still in bed. Her voice, more whiny than usual this morning, came thin and high through the open door. 'Fra-a-a-ank!'

'Just a minute!'

'Fra-a-a-ank!' she insisted.

Frank was tearing his way through a piece of toast, washed down by a too-hot cup of tea. 'Ugh! Burnt a hole through me throat! Get a needle and sew it up for me, Kate, will you?'

'*Frank*!' Kate's face registered horror.

Frank leaned over to put an arm round her shoulder. 'All right, only joking! You didn't think I meant it, did you?'

'Fra-a-ank!'

'Put a sock in it, you!' called Mum, from the kitchen. 'We all got our hands full out here. Nothing important, of course. Only like getting ready to earn our living. Minor details like that.'

'Any more tea in the pot?' called Dad, from the other bedroom.

'There goes another one!' said Mum. 'A duet, now. Good as Top of the Pops, innit! Kate, come on and make your packed lunch!'

'I'm just tidying my bed.'

'You making a meal of that today, ain't you?' said Frank, grinning. 'That's the third time you folded that duvet!'

In fact, it was the fourth time. She had folded

and unfolded the duvet, with its pattern of pink and yellow flowers, while she made up her mind, and unmade it again. She had chosen that cover herself; she had chosen it with delight, now she began to hate it. She would go, she wouldn't go. Yes, no, yes, no. How could she put the sign up anyway, with Frank in the room to see? 'Aren't you going to be late for work?' Kate hinted.

'Have a heart!' said Frank. 'Do you want me to choke?'

'No but – I thought you have to be early. You said it's important to be early when you're on price work.' Usually she watched him go with a little pang – a whole long day before she would see him again! And today she couldn't wait to get him out of the house! Kate felt extra guilty because she was deceiving Frank, who was always so kind to her.

All the same, her legs took her to the window. That didn't mean she'd made up her mind, of course. It just meant she was going to the window.

'Yeah, right, right! Mustn't be late!' Frank rushed into the bedroom to give Dawn a last hug, then back to the sitting room for a last mouthful of toast. 'What you doing with them curtains, Kate? Right, see you later!'

Full of guilt, Kate straightened the curtain. From the window, she watched Frank's back receding. I want to do it and I *don't* want to do it, she thought. I want to do it because it will be an exciting adventure, and it will make Desmond happy. But I *don't* want to do it because it's a more wrong thing than I ever did before, and I can get in a lot of trouble. . . . And it seems like I can't make up my mind.

With hands that seemed to move of their own

accord, Kate hitched up the curtain again. Then she ran out of the room, quite frightened by the hitched-up curtain, and the decision she had apparently made.

In the passage, Kate collided with Mum. Mum was going into the sitting room, and there was no way of stopping her. 'Who's been messing up these curtains?' Kate heard. She waited till Mum went into the bathroom, then slipped back to hitch the curtain up once again. Her heart was beating faster, and there was a swimmy feeling in her head.

'Kate!' called Mum again, from the bathroom. 'I don't believe you done that packed lunch yet! You planning to go hungry, then? You on a fast? You got the anorexia, or something?'

'Just coming!' called Kate. 'Coming, coming, coming!'

As she was making her sandwiches, Dad padded out of the bedroom in his dressing gown, and coughed his way into the sitting room to put the television on. When Kate went in for her school bag, the curtain had been pulled down. 'Wish people wouldn't ruck up them curtains,' he complained. 'Them curtains supposed to give us a bit of privacy. I mean, can't have every Tom, Dick and Harry getting their eyeful!'

'Don't you think you should go back to bed?' said Kate, through the buzzing in her head. 'And take a proper care of that cough?'

'Got to have a *bit* of pleasure, haven't I?' he reproached her. 'By the way, any more tea in the pot?'

'He's had his tea!' called Mum, banging out to work. 'And his breakfast. And don't nobody wait on Lady Muck in there, she can get her own!'

Too late, it occurred to Kate that she could just as well have arranged to meet Desmond outside anyway, and told him her decision then. Whichever was first out could have waited for the other at the corner. As things were, she didn't know whether Desmond had seen her signal or not. He might have passed by at the wrong time. Sometimes he went to school early, and sometimes later, there was no telling. So he might be at school already, and the chance missed.

And good if that happened, Kate thought, because I didn't want to do it anyway, not really. . . . I don't *think* I did. It was like my hand put that curtain up all by itself. . . . So I shall go straight to school, and bad luck if Desmond saw the curtain, because I changed my mind and I don't want to bunk off after all.

Actually though, actually, you can't do that, can you! If you promise a person you're going to do something, you have to do it, don't you? So I think I have to go to Somerset Gardens whether I like it or not, and see if Desmond's there.

The troubled thoughts pounded in Kate's head as she sped down the road.

If he's not there, I can go straight to school like I said, and not get in trouble for bunking off.

. . . He's not there, I can't see him! Hooray, Desmond's not there! I don't have to do that wrong thing I can get in trouble for!

. . . Yes he is, though, he is there! Hiding round the corner like yesterday, I just saw his head.

Oh well, that's it. That's it, and it's all decided, and it's no use worrying any more. It's no use worrying, because it's done now, and anyway it will

93

be a good adventure. Hooray, I'm going to have an exciting adventure, today!

By the time she rounded the corner, there was a bright beam of welcome on Kate's face for Desmond.

There was no answering greeting from him. Roughly, he seized Kate by the arm and dragged her across the street. 'Come on! Quick, get behind the wall!' And he kept his face averted because otherwise the hope, the great hope, might show!

'What's the hurry?' said Kate. 'That burglar can't see us; he's not at his gate yet.'

'Somebody from school might come, dum-dum,' said Desmond. 'And tell.'

'Oh.'

They sat in silence. They sat, and sat, and sat. And the pale winter sun rose above the houses, picking out shiny dustbins, and yellow bricks, grimy with age. 'It's quite a nice day, isn't it?' said Kate, politely. 'Not so cold, and a little bit sunny.'

'Shut up,' said Desmond. 'Don't talk less you have to, somebody might hear.'

'You didn't say that before.'

'Well I'm saying it now, so just belt up!'

'All right, *be* like that!' Kate's feelings were not hurt. This was just Desmond, being his usual self. It didn't mean anything; you didn't have to take any notice.

Time dragged. 'I got my packed lunch,' said Kate.

'I said don't talk!'

'It's a bit boring here, though. I thought it would be exciting but it isn't, it's boring.'

'You don't have to blame me.'

'And anyway, I thought you would be glad we won't be hungry.'

'All right, I'm glad we won't be hungry. Now shut up, can't you!'

'Don't tell me to shut up. I made an extra sandwich for you, because I know you have school dinners.'

'Did you?'

'I just said so.'

'Yeah, well. . . . All right, thanks!'

'That's better. That's more better manners. Anyway I don't see why we can't whisper, there's nobody to hear. Now everybody's gone to school there isn't nobody in the whole street. It's like there's nobody in the whole world. And I don't think nothing's going to happen, neither.'

'Say that again!' said Desmond, suddenly.

'Say what again?'

'Say nothing's going to happen.'

'Why? What for?'

'When you said it yesterday, that's when those blokes come down the road!'

Kate beamed at him. 'I see! You mean I can be magic! All right, I'll see if it works this time. *Nothing's going to happen, nothing's going to happen, nothing's going to happen*.' She closed her eyes and screwed up her face, concentrating hard while she said the magic words again, and again, and again. She opened her eyes and squinted. 'Has it worked yet?'

'Look!' said Desmond. Kate raised her head cautiously, and peeped over the wall. The scruffy man from yesterday, still unshaven, had just emerged from his front door.

'He's going up the road!' whispered Kate. *Now* it was getting to be exciting!

'All right, I'm not blind.'

'Shall we follow him?'

'In a minute. Wait till he gets round the corner. . . . *Now*!'

The children sprinted along the pavement. Desmond's legs were like piston rods, carrying him farther and farther from Kate. She gasped, and there was a pain in her side from trying to keep up. She was anxious as well. Scruffy had turned into Devonshire Road, which was a short one, and even Desmond might not be in time to see which way he went. He could go right or left into Wessex Road, they wouldn't know which, or he could go into a house, and they wouldn't see.

At the corner, Desmond waited for Kate. 'What's the matter with you? You run too slow!'

There was no answer to that, and anyway Kate couldn't make one, because she was fighting for breath. She peeped round the corner and saw Scruffy's figure at the far end, just turning left. In spite of his unkempt appearance he walked with a swagger, his head held back, cock of the walk.

Again, the children ran. 'Look!' said Desmond.

In the next road, Scruffy was lounging against the bus stop. Kate stared in dismay. They hadn't thought of that. They hadn't thought he might get on a bus!

'Have you got any money?' said Desmond.

'No.' She wanted to say 'Have you?' but lacked the breath.

'Look!' said Desmond, desperately. 'The bus!'

His hope was being snatched from him. In his mind's eye he saw it going, whisked away into the

winter sunshine on a red London bus. He grabbed
Kate's wrist and dragged her with him to the end
of the queue. Have to risk being seen! The bus
drew up and people began to get on. It was a
Routemaster bus – the sort where you get on at the
back, and buy your ticket from the conductor. 'Seats
on top,' said the conductor. Scruffy went upstairs,
and Desmond pushed Kate inside. The bus was
quite full. Perhaps the conductor would forget to
ask them for their money.

He was coming now. 'Any more fares?' Desmond
pointed vaguely towards the front of the bus, indicating that somewhere up there was an adult who
would be responsible for paying his fare and Kate's.
The conductor moved on. Kate felt very daring,
and wicked. This was getting to be a *fine* adventure.

The bus pulled up at the next stop, and the
conductor moved back to supervise the getting on
and off. 'Change seats!' said Desmond. 'Muddle
him up!'

Outwitting the grown-ups now! A fine adventure
indeed! They moved to fresh places, one behind the
other.

The conductor moved forward again. He looked
at the children and then towards the front of the
bus, as though trying to remember if anyone had
paid for them. A large woman had seated herself
beside Kate, pinning her in. The conductor took
the large woman's fare, and looked at Kate once
more. Kate began to feel nervous. Outwitting the
grown-ups was all very well, but you could get into
trouble, couldn't you?

The conductor had passed them now; they were
looking at his back. Desmond prodded Kate from
behind, and when she turned, she saw him with

one foot on the stairs, evidently about to climb. Flustered, Kate kneed and elbowed the large woman, as she struggled to get past. 'Don't mind me!' said the large woman, crossly.

Kate's nervousness grew. Fear gathered in the dark corners of her mind, threatening to spoil this lovely exciting day. Firmly, she tried to suppress it. What was the matter with that large woman, anyway? Didn't she know that here were two children having an important adventure?

With difficulty, because of the moving bus, Kate followed Desmond on to the upper deck. He had found a seat at the back, right by the stairs, and Kate fell into the place beside him. He gripped her arm, and his finger pointed towards the front where Scruffy sat, next to a smelly-looking tramp. Scruffy was edging farther and farther from the tramp; finally he stood up, and turned. His eyes (and they *were* shifty) swept round the bus.

'He seen us, now!' said Kate, dismayed.

'Shut up!' said Desmond. 'He's just looking to sit somewhere else.'

Scruffy swayed towards them, and re-seated himself three places up.

'But he *seen* us!'

'Don't matter. We're just two kids on a bus, that's all. He don't know we're following him. You are so stupid sometimes, Frog!'

'But you said before—'

'That was before. . . . Don't go on about what I said before! You keep going on about what I said before.'

'Oh.' A thought struck her. 'Desmond, if you say something one time, doesn't it count for another time?'

'What you on about now?'

'You said you would look after me before, doesn't that count for now?'

'Course it does!'

'But you said it *before*. Like you said about him seeing us *before*.'

'That is a completely different thing.'

'Is it?'

'Yes, it is.'

'I don't understand.'

'Bad luck!'

The conductor ran up the stairs with practised feet. 'Tickets?' he said to Desmond.

'My mum got them,' Desmond tried. 'Downstairs.'

'Don't come that with me!' said the conductor. 'I know what you're up to. You been dodging about changing seats ever since you got on the bus.'

'Got to get off now,' said Desmond, seizing Kate's wrist and dragging her to the stairs. The bus gave a lurch just then, and Kate lost her balance, knocking her head against the rail. Now *that* wasn't supposed to be part of the adventure, was it?

'Little perishers!' said the conductor, angrily. 'Wait for the stop now, don't you get off while it's moving!'

'Come on,' said Desmond, to Kate. He thumped down the stairs, and Kate followed. The school bag dragged on her arm, and got in her way. It was all right for Desmond – he had no bag to hamper him. He brought his swimming things, once a week, in a plastic carrier; and if there was homework, which was not often, he mostly stuck the books under his coat.

The bus pulled up at the stop. 'Let them off first!' called the conductor, from the top of the stairs.

Kate moved to get off the bus. 'Where d'you think you're going?' said Desmond, grabbing at her. The children squeezed into the luggage space, while the new lot of passengers climbed aboard. The bus moved off once more. 'I think this is Hillesden High Street,' said Kate. 'We're ever such a long way from home, how we going to get back?'

'Shut up!' said Desmond. 'Look!'

He was coming. Lurching down the stairs, arrogant as though he owned the bus, came the person they were following.

He stood on the platform, swinging nonchalantly by the rail. Behind him, Kate and Desmond squeezed deeper into the luggage space. The bus trundled on, then stopped behind a lorry that was holding it up. And Scruffy jumped off.

'Come on!' said Desmond.

'No!' said Kate, frightened the bus might suddenly move again.

'All right,' said Desmond. 'Stay there!'

He jumped. He was off the bus, and she was still on it. Kate's head, already throbbing because of the bump, now spun with indecision. The bus gave a little jerk. It was going to move, it was moving!

Kate jumped, anyway.

She staggered, partly regained her balance, lost it again, and toppled over. Now she had grazed knees to add to the bump on her head. 'You do really mad things sometimes!' said Desmond, unkindly.

'Silly little girl!' scolded a passer-by.

'Drop dead!' Desmond snarled at the passer-by. 'Come on Kate. He went that way.'

They ran, because they were in a street with a lot of shops, and a lot of shoppers, and it was going to be only too easy to lose Scruffy. Now and again they caught sight of his head, bobbing away amongst the other heads. He stopped to look in a shop window, and they stopped too. He moved on, and they moved. He stopped again. The children dodged into another shop entrance, and peeped out to see what he did.

He was moving off again – swaggering, his head held back like before. He turned into a side street, and the children turned. Round the corner, unexpectedly, he was waiting for them!

His hand shot out, and he grabbed Desmond by the arm. 'What's the game, then?' His voice was harsh, the twisted expression horribly menacing.

'Nothing,' said Desmond. 'Let go of me.'

I'm not going to run, Kate thought, wildly. I'm going to be brave, and stay with Desmond! Her heart was racing, though, her thoughts approaching panic.

'You're tailing me. What for?' The grip on Desmond's arm tightened, painfully.

'Nothing. I ain't.'

'Don't give me that! You was on the bus, I see you. I seen you round where I live, as well. And I don't want to see you no more, so push off!'

'Get you!' Desmond sneered, defiantly. He stepped back smartly though, when Scruffy released his arm and marched away, swaggering up the road.

'Oh, Desmond!' said Kate.

'All right, all right, no big deal!'

'It was a lucky escape, though,' said Kate, thankfully. She stood watching Scruffy's rapidly retreating back, marvelling at the lucky escape they had had.

Desmond scowled, and shrugged.

'He didn't do nothing to us! I can't believe it!'

'Come on!' Desmond urged her.

'Come on where?'

'After him, of course.'

'After *him*?'

'I thought you want to catch the burglar.'

She *had* wanted to, but she didn't now. She wanted to go home. She wanted to be at school. The day, which had started out an exciting game, had turned into something like a nightmare.

'Are you coming, or not?'

'I'm coming, I suppose,' said Kate, in a small voice.

I think I might have made a mistake, she thought. When I went off detecting before I think I should not have changed my mind. I don't think I'm any good at dangerous things, I don't think I'm cut out for it. And Desmond said he would look after me, but I don't think he is doing it very well.

Look at all the unkind things he did! He ran ahead, and forgot all about me, and I couldn't keep up. And I bumped myself twice, and I don't think he cared a bit! I don't think I'm cut out for being brave, and I don't think Desmond is cut out for looking after people.

Oh, well . . . give it one more try, I suppose, and see what happens!

Shaken but recovering, Kate ploughed after Desmond. The shops were getting left behind; there were no more shop entrances to dodge into, only the fronts of people's houses. The children followed more warily, ready to dive into private property if

102

necessary — but they needn't have bothered, because, surprisingly enough, Scruffy did not look back once.

There was a large building ahead, with people going in and out. Sharply, and unexpectedly, Scruffy also turned into the building. 'What is it?' said Kate.

Desmond did not answer. Kate squinted at him sideways, and saw that his face was a mask of fury. 'What is it?' said Kate again.

Desmond was speechless with the rage of frustration.

'Desmond—'

'Oh, belt up!'

'No!' said Kate, with spirit. 'I won't belt up! Who do you think you are, Desmond Locke, telling me to belt up? What's the matter?'

'All right,' said Desmond, savagely, 'I'll tell you what's the matter! He tricked us! We come all this way for nothing, that's what's the matter!'

'What do you mean?'

'See that place he went in? Know what it is?'

'No.'

'It's only the dole place, innit! He's only just come to sign on, hasn't he?'

Kate laughed, in sudden joy.

'Glad you think it's so funny!'

'I don't think it's exactly funny, but I think it's mostly good, because now we can go home.'

Desmond kicked at the nearest wall.

'We can, can't we, Desmond? We can go home now, can't we!'

Desmond went on kicking at the wall.

'Shut up, I'm thinking!'

'All right, Desmond,' said Kate, aimiably. 'You

think! I will just sit here on this step while you think, and have a little rest.'

'He could be going to do it after,' said Desmond.

'Do what after?'

'Meet the gang, and do the burglary. He could be going to do it after.'

'You don't mean . . . ?' The smile on Kate's face faded.

'Yes I do. Course I do. We got to wait for him to come out, innit, and follow him again!'

'Oh.'

'You don't want to, do you?'

'Not much.'

'All right then, you go home!'

'Shall I?'

'I don't care if you go. It's nothing to me if you go.'

Kate put a piece of hair into her mouth, and chewed it. Could she? Should she? It would be a lonely thing to do, but she wasn't enjoying it here. It was a great pity Desmond didn't want her any more, though, because it had been very nice to be wanted.

'Are you going then?' said Desmond, roughly.

Kate squinted at Desmond sideways, wrinkling her nose so the glasses bounced up and down. It will be lonely for him too if I go, she thought. Perhaps if I just sit here he will realize it, and change his mind, and want me again after all.

'Well . . .'

Kate went on sitting.

'That Scruffy can be a long time, you know,' said Desmond. 'Coming out – he can be a long time. You have to queue up in there, it can be a very long queue.'

104

'Don't matter.'

'You can go home if you like.'

'. . . Would you rather if I go, then?'

'It's up to you.'

'But do you *want* me to stay?'

'. . . What do you think?'

'I think you want me to, a bit.'

'So what you ask for, if you know?'

'You do, then!'

'I said what do you ask for, if you know?'

'We have to agree on something, though,' said Kate. 'We have to agree to let each other off, if we do something wrong.'

Desmond shrugged, again.

'All right?'

'. . . Yeah, all right.'

'I mean it, you know.'

'All right, I said it, didn't I? I said it, what more do you want?'

'Nothing more. That is all I want, Desmond. I don't want any more at all.' She drew a sudden sharp breath. 'Look! Look who's just now come!'

Emerging from the dole place was not Scruffy but one of the others. The one Desmond said was bad news. He was dressed in leathers, and walking rapidly towards the children. Desmond seized the back of Kate's neck, and twisted it roughly towards the wall.

'Ow!'

'Keep still! Wait till he's past!'

'Are we going to follow *him* now then, Desmond?'

'Course we are!'

Kate swallowed her fears, and made a valiant effort to get back into the spirit of it.

7

In trouble

Bad News loped along towards the shops, and the children followed, keeping a good distance. 'We must make sure this one don't see us,' said Kate. 'We must make extra special sure this time, mustn't we, Desmond? We must, mustn't we!'

'Shut up!'

'He's gone, though!' said Kate, in sudden dismay. 'I lost sight of him!'

'That's because you talk too much.'

'Did you see where he went?'

'No, I didn't. You made me not look, Frog. You talk too much, and you made me not look.'

'He must have went in somewhere.'

'Brilliant!'

'All right, you don't have to be so sarcastic. Let's just look in all the shops.'

Without waiting for Kate, Desmond began to run. He slowed down at roughly the spot where Bad News had disappeared, and Kate caught up with him, panting. 'I think I know where he is,' said Desmond.

'Where, then?'

'In this pub.'

'Shall we go in?'

'Kids ain't allowed. . . . We could peep!'

'I'll do it,' said Kate, to make up for talking too much. She pushed open the heavy door, and peered round the dark, smoke-filled room. 'I can't see him,' she said, pulling her head back.

'Look again.'

Kate looked. 'I don't think they're very nice people in there,' she said. 'I don't like the look of any of them, actually. And it doesn't smell very nice, besides!'

'Probably a villains' hang-out!'

'Do you think so?' said Kate, in awe. She pushed open the door again, to have a good look at the villains' hang-out while she had the chance. . . . Then her head came back sharply, and two high spots of colour burned in her face.

'Is he there, then?' said Desmond.

'Yes, but I have to go, I have to hide!' She glanced around her wildly.

Desmond pulled her into the doorway of an adjacent shop. 'It's all right. What's the matter with you? We can hide here. Follow him again, when he comes out.'

'I'm not talking about *him*, I'm talking about *him*.'

'You *are* mad, Frog!'

'No, I'm not, then. It's Frank. He's in there as well.'

'Who's Frank?'

'*You* know! You know my sister Dawn. Well, her husband. That lives in our house now. Haven't you never seen him in the road?'

'Oh yeah, I think I know the one.'

'I'm scared he'll see me. I shall have to go.'

She made to run into the shop, but Desmond grabbed her arm. 'No, hold on! He wouldn't tell your mum, would he?'

'He might let it out to my sister, and I think she would *like* to tell.'

'I bet she wouldn't. *My* sister wouldn't.'

'Your sister is not my sister. Let go my arm, Desmond.'

He pushed her from him, roughly. 'All right, go on then! Go and hide in the shop. Go home if you like. It don't matter to me!'

Kate chewed frantically at a piece of hair.

'I can do it without you, you know. Do you think I can't do it without you?'

'Look out, he's coming!' Kate bolted into the shop, which was a fashion boutique, packed with rails full of skirts and tops and dresses. Frank was not likely to come in here! Kate cowered behind some jazzy orange and black creations, and wondered how long before it would be safe to come out.

A hand grabbed her wrist, and yanked her from her hiding place. 'It's all right, he's gone!' said Desmond.

'Are you sure?'

'I said so, didn't I? I followed him. And there was another one. One with all spots on his face. They went off in a little van.'

'Oh.' Fright receded.

'So can we get on with it now? What we come to do?'

'I thought you said you could do it without me.'

'. . . I didn't mean it, did I!'

'. . . Anyway, he might have gone already. We might have missed him. It's not my fault if we missed him. I didn't *ask* you to come in this shop and find me!'

'Who said it's your fault? Did I say anything about your fault? Anyway, I don't think he will have gone yet, he has to have time to drink his beer.'

'Oh yeah, that's right. . . . Desmond, perhaps this pub is the meeting place.'

'That's what I was thinking.'

'Be careful – Scruffy could be coming along soon!'

'And we don't want them to see us.'

They waited, and waited, and waited. Suddenly Kate gave a squeal. 'No, it's not the meeting place, it's not the meeting place. He's coming out. Look!'

'Great stuff! Come on, follow behind!'

They dodged amongst the shopping crowds to the end of the block, and round a corner. There, between two parked cars, was a shiny motor bike. Here Bad News stopped, unlocked the box at the back, and took out a helmet. 'Oh, no!' said Desmond furiously.

The motorbike sputtered and roared. With disappointed eyes, the children watched it out of sight.

'So what shall we do now?' said Kate. 'Shall we go back to that dole place?'

'Might as well.'

'Probably Scruffy's gone too though, by now. Probably he got to the end of the queue. He probably got on another bus, and went home.'

'Great stuff!' said Desmond bitterly. 'Great detecting!'

They trailed back without much hope. They sat on a step, outside the dole place, while a sun with no warmth in it streamed over them, out of an ice blue sky. 'Say "nothing's going to happen" again,' Desmond suggested.

Kate closed her eyes and said 'nothing's going to happen' with great earnestness, over and over. 'Has it worked yet?' she asked, without opening them.

'Nah!'

'Do you know something?' said Kate.

'What?'

'I don't think he's in there any more.'

'Brilliant!'

'Do you think we should give up?'

Desmond shrugged.

'Actually, I want to go to the toilet,' said Kate.

'Go on, then.'

'Only I'm afraid you won't wait for me.'

'Please yourself.'

'So what shall we do now? Wait a bit longer?'

'Nah! I'm fed up of waiting!' Morosely, Desmond kicked at the step with the heel of one shabby trainer.

'I think it's going to be a long time till half past three. Till they come out of school, and we can go to our house,' said Kate.

Desmond shrugged.

'I know,' said Kate brightly, 'we could go to the park. There's toilets in the park.'

'Nah!'

Desmond got up suddenly and mooched off down the road. Kate followed, at his elbow. 'So where we going, then?'

'Home, innit!'

'Are we going to walk all the way?'

Desmond ignored her.

'Ain't you going to talk to me?' said Kate, with a sigh.

'Isn't nothing to talk about.'

'Ain't we going to do any more detecting, then?' The frightening things that had happened seemed a long way away, now. Anyway – had they been so very dreadful? In memory they didn't seem so.

110

Perhaps she was getting to be a bit brave after all. She would be truly disappointed now, Kate found, if there were to be no more adventures.

Desmond shrugged. What was the use of trying? They had tried, and failed, and what was the use of going through all that again?

'Anyway, never mind. Perhaps the police will catch the burglar soon.'

Desmond shrugged once more.

'And everyone will know it's not your dad just the same. Just the same as if *we* caught him.'

'It's all right for you!'

Something in Desmond's tone made Kate run forward, and peer anxiously into his face. To her surprise and consternation, she saw that two great tears were rolling down his cheeks. 'Don't cry!'

'I'm not.'

'Yes you are, I see you!'

'Don't look, then. You not supposed to look!'

'All right, then, I won't. I won't look at you crying, because you don't want me to. Is that all right?'

'And I don't want to hear your voice neither! Yacketty yacketty, yack, yack, yack!'

Kate fell back a few steps, and followed Desmond with a troubled face. His pain hurt her too, and she ached to comfort him, but he didn't seem to want her comfort; he wanted her to pretend she hadn't seen. And I hope the police find the burglar today, she thought, fiercely! I hope they find him today, and lock him up in prison, so Desmond will not have any more crying to hide.

And it is a pity if he won't speak to me now, because it can be a very miserable thing to be with somebody who won't speak to you. All those hours!

And besides that, somebody else that knows us might see us out of school. We should have stayed in Hillesden really, it would have been more better.

In silence, they dragged two weary, uncomfortable miles.

Before they reached Wessex Road, Desmond turned off sharply, without looking round. 'Wait for me! Desmond, wait for me!'

Desmond trudged on.

'Where we going, though?'

'Where you think? There's toilets in the park!'

Once in the play area, Desmond pushed Kate on to the roundabout and began running with it – faster and faster and faster, as though his legs were not worn out with walking, as though the running would free him from the dark feelings which clawed at him, deep inside.

Kate squealed with pleasure. It was good to be doing something fun for a change. Desmond leapt on to the roundabout with her, and they careered wildly round, the sharp air tingling their faces and catching in their lungs, while the last of the cold yellow sunshine slanted through the bare trees.

Kate was tired though, if Desmond wasn't. They sat in the shelter, and shared Kate's sandwiches. When some policemen walked through the park they crouched under the seats and hid, giggling, until the police had passed. Her energies renewed, Kate ran to the swings, and Desmond ran after her. 'Let's see who can get highest,' said Kate, recklessly.

She stood on the seat, and pushed with her feet. Higher and higher. The chains jerked and looped. Kate was frightened, but excitement drove her on.

'Stop!' said Desmond, suddenly.

'I'm winning you!'

'Stop!' Desmond slowed his own swing, and grabbed at Kate's as it passed, to hold it back. 'That's dangerous!'

'What's the matter with you? We done much more dangerous things than that today.' The madness was over, though, the excitement draining away.

'That's different,' said Desmond.

'How is it different?'

Desmond pondered. '. . . All right, I'll tell you. The other things were *necessary*, see what I mean? Like if you hurt yourself on the swing it would be for nothing, wouldn't it?'

'Oh, right!' That was more like it, Desmond was really looking after her, at last! She gave him a bright beam of gratitude.

They played sensibly after that, enjoying it. A few small children appeared with their mothers, then some older ones began to come. School was out. 'Home now!' said Desmond.

'I've had a *great* day,' said Kate.

'Run though,' said Desmond. 'And turn away your face 'case we see anybody from our class.'

She had almost forgotten they were doing something naughty.

'You just missed her,' said Dawn. She looked pleased about something.

'Missed who?' said Kate.

'Your mate. Suzette. She come to the door. 'Bout five minutes ago.'

'*What?*'

'She come to find out why you wasn't in school. She was missing you. They went to the library and she didn't have a partner. She was really upset about it. Got herself in a real state!'

'You're a naughty girl, Kate,' said Dad, 'You been a really naughty girl!'

Kate hung her head. 'I know.'

'What's your mum going to say?' The last part of Dad's sentence ended in a spluttering cough.

'You won't tell her, will you?' Kate pleaded.

'. . . I don't suppose so. You been a naughty girl, though!'

'*You* won't tell her, Dawn, will you?'

'That depends,' said Dawn.

'Depends on what?'

'You will have to be my slave.'

'All right, I don't mind, I'll be your slave. . . . How long do I have to be your slave for?'

'Till I say you can stop,' said Dawn, greatly enjoying herself. 'You can do the washing up for a start. And you have to tell Mum it was me that done it.'

Kate fell over her feet to oblige. 'Anything else?' she said humbly, coming back.

'Make the beds,' said Dawn. 'Both of them.'

'That's supposed to be your job, though. For your exercise.'

'I didn't have time,' said Dawn, rearranging herself and her lump, to get a better view of the telly.

'You're just lazy,' said Kate.

'Don't be like that, Kate,' said Dad.

'You have to be respectful,' said Dawn, 'as well as my slave. And when you done the beds, you can go up the road and get me a bar of chocolate. Which you can pay for with your money,' she added. It was great to have power. Dawn had no scruples

114

about using her new power to the utmost advantage.

'Dad. . . .' Kate appealed.

Dad shifted uncomfortably. 'Leave me out of it. Anyway, you have been a naughty girl, you know.'

Kate swallowed. There was no getting away from it, she *had* been very naughty. She had done something very naughty indeed, and it had got found out, and Mum wasn't going to let her off this one! Dawn was being a pig, and Dad was letting her do it, but those weren't the important things. The important thing was to stop Dawn telling, if she could.

Dawn was just cramming the last morsel of chocolate into her mouth when Mum came in.

'What you scoffing chocolate for?'

'I'm not!'

'What's this wrapper, then? Christmas decoration?'

'It's nothing to do with me,' said Dad.

'You know you ain't supposed to have chocolate,' said Mum. 'You know the clinic said you're putting on too much weight!'

'I can't help that,' said Dawn, caressing her lump. 'Most of that's the baby.'

'Oh? You planning to have a two stone baby, then? You aiming for the Guinness Book of Records?'

'The chocolate was a present, actually,' said Dawn. 'From Kate. Was I supposed to not eat it, then? And hurt her feelings?'

'What you giving presents to Lady Muck for?' said Mum, suspiciously.

'It's nothing to do with me,' said Dad.

'What isn't?' said Mum.

115

'Leave me out of it,' said Dad.

'Leave you out of what?'

'It's between Dawn and Kate,' said Dad. 'It's nothing to do with me.'

'You ought to have more sense anyway,' Mum scolded Dawn. 'How you reckon you're going to look after a baby, if you can't even look after yourself properly?' Mum was late home tonight, worn out, and more than ready to pick on the first person who displeased her. 'Have you taken them things to the launderette I asked you to? No, of course you haven't! You're waiting for them to get up out of that basket and take theirselves! Which judging from the pong off of your dad's socks, they might very well do!'

'I haven't had time,' Dawn muttered.

'Oh? What you been doing all day, then? Come on, what? Come on, you fat lazy cow, you! Starting with nine o'clock this morning, what you been doing?'

'You wanna ask Kate what *she's* been doing!' Dawn blurted out, cringing from Mum's attack.

'Why?'

'You ask her!'

'She in trouble at school? You in trouble at school, Kate?'

Kate trembled.

'All right, don't tell me, I don't want to know. Right, Madam Dawn! As I was saying – what time did you manage to fall out of bed this morning? Or should I say this afternoon? And don't tell me about that pain again! I don't want to hear no more about that pain that comes and goes when it suits you.'

'She hasn't *been* to school,' Dawn blurted out, to take Mum's attention off herself.

116

'What!'

'She hasn't *been* to school. Kate hasn't been to school. She bunked off today. And you think *I'm* the bad one,' Dawn added, virtuously.

'It's nothing to do with me,' said Dad.

'That's right!' said Mum, turning on him furiously. 'You're going to leave it all to me, as usual! Good job *somebody* in this house cares what their kid gets up to! What you do it for, Kate? Come on, what you do it for? What for!'

'I don't know.'

'Oh? Who does know, then, the man in the moon?'

'Suzette wasn't in it,' said Dawn, helpfully. 'I do know that.'

'Shut up, you! I bet *I* know who was in it! Master Locke the burglar's son! Wasn't it! Wasn't it! Answer me, Kate! You want your head looked at, you know that? The very idea, to go mixing yourself up with that scum-bag! Are you listening to me? Well look at me, then! Here! I'm here, not hanging off of the ceiling. So now, let's have the rest of it. Where you been all day?'

'. . . Playing in the park.'

'Not good enough. Try again.'

'. . . Looking for burglars,' said Kate, in a low voice.

'Have you lost *all* your marbles? Here's me thinking you're safe in school, and instead of that you're out on the streets asking for every sort of trouble going.'

'I was all right. Desmond was looking after me.'

Mum slapped Kate, hard, on the legs. 'Don't talk so stupid!' She slapped her again. 'Don't let me hear you talk so stupid!' She went to add a third

117

slap, and Kate dodged, to avoid the blow. The blow landed on the side of one of the dining chairs; the pain in Mum's hand was agonizing. Pain and fury blotted out reason, and Mum began hitting Kate in real earnest.

Kate cried. 'I'm sorry, I'm sorry, I won't do it again!'

There was the sound of a key turning in the front door. In great high spirits, Frank bounced into the room. 'Hey! What's happened to the happy home?'

'Mind your own business!' said Mum, hitting Kate again.

Kate's cries rose to a bellow.

'Fire!' said Frank. 'The house is on fire, I can smell it!'

'Where?' said Dad, alarmed.

'Nowhere,' said Dawn, through the rest of the din. 'It's just Frank being funny.'

'Water!' said Frank, and he dashed into the kitchen. He came back with a bucket, and brandished it in front of Mum. 'You're burning, you're burning!'

'Leave off!' said Mum. 'It's no joke, this!' But her mouth twitched at the corners, her anger beginning to evaporate.

'Shall I?' said Frank, pretending to aim the non-existent contents of the bucket at Mum's head.

'Give over!' said Mum, laughing properly now.

Frank swung the bucket, and stood back to admire the supposed effect. He giggled, and his eyes swivelled towards the bucket. 'Well, what do you know! Silly me! I forgot to fill it!'

'The fire's out now, anyway,' said Kate, beaming.

'True facts. Good job I got a strong nose,' said Frank.

'Probably Dad's socks you smelled!' said Mum.

'Always fussing over Kate!' Dawn muttered, sulkily.

The sofa had been pulled forward as usual, in the late evening, to make room for Kate's blow-up bed. Kate turned under the duvet. She had been trying to get to sleep for an hour and a half. It was always hard to get to sleep with the light still on, and the grown-ups whispering and coughing, even though they did turn the telly down for her.

Kate peered round the end of the sofa. Frank was still there, the last one up. He was sitting in the armchair, whistling to himself, and jiggling something in his pocket.

'Frank?' Kate whispered.

'You go to sleep!' said Frank.

'I want to say thank you, though. I want to say thank you, for saving me from Mum.'

Frank ran his fingers through the yellow curls. 'Any time! . . . What was it all about, anyway?'

'I did something bad.'

'How bad?'

'The worst thing in my life.'

'Like what?'

'I bunked off school.' It *had* been a disgraceful thing to do. She felt really guilty about it now. Looking for burglars was no excuse; she didn't even feel like mentioning that part.

Frank grinned. 'That's nothing!'

'Isn't it?'

'Nah – I done it a load of times.'

'Did you?' A warm feeling began to flow through Kate. She felt comforted, supported. *Darling* Frank – he always knew the right thing to say!

'Yeah – bunking off's nothing. Everybody bunks off some time in their life.'

Kate wasn't quite sure about that one, but she was grateful to Frank for saying it. The warm feeling was all round her now, soothing her troubled conscience, lifting the load of guilt. Love welled up till it hurt, in her chest. Across the room, Kate beamed her love at Frank.

But she felt guilty about something else now. She wouldn't feel happy until she confessed it. 'I saw you today, you know.'

'Did you?'

'In Hillesden High Street, in a pub.'

'Is *that* where you got to, on your day off? Yeah, I was there – having me break. Having a drink with a mate. I didn't see *you*.'

'I ran away from you,' said Kate, in a low voice. She searched his face anxiously, looking for signs of reproach; but without her glasses, the image she saw was blurred and smudged, so she couldn't properly read his expression.

'Ran away from *me*?'

'I thought you might tell . . . well, I thought you might tell Dawn.'

'*Kate*! You know me better than that! I wouldn't have give you away, I wouldn't have told *anybody*!'

'I know,' said Kate, remorsefully. 'Can you forgive me?'

Frank giggled. 'Oh, come and have a cuddle. Come on, Funny-face, just a quick one before I go to bed.'

Kate crawled out of bed and joined Frank in the armchair. She felt his comforting arm round her shoulders. 'You've forgiven me, then?'

'Pack it in! I'd probably forgive you anything!'

Kate sighed with contentment. 'Do you know something, Frank?'

'What's that?'

'I don't know what I'd do without you!'

8

A terrible shock

'What's the matter?' said Mum. 'You look like a wet week.'

'I haven't got a letter,' said Kate miserably. 'For Mrs Warren. About why I was away.'

'Oh well, that's your lookout. You should have thought of that before.'

'Come on, Ma!' Frank wheedled. 'Be a sport, eh?' He put his head on one side, and smiled his most winning smile.

'You'd charm the birds off the trees, you would!' Mum accused him. 'All right, Kate, just this once. I'll say you were sick. Which you were, anyway, in the mental department!'

In the playground, Natasha was crying. Florence and Ranjit ministered to her, their arms twined uncomfortably around her neck. Kate reassured herself that the precious note was still in her bag, then gave her attention to the rare sight of Natasha in tears.

There was another unusual sight in the playground that morning. Today, the other members of the Super Six were in a group apart, comforting Marie who was also crying. From time to time, Marie's group cast baleful glances at Natasha's group. Clearly there had been a quarrel. What about?

In the classroom, the tears continued to flow.

'Whatever is the matter with you two?' said Mrs Warren, impatiently.

'It's not funny, Mrs Warren,' said Ranjit. 'Natasha's house been burgled!'

'Oh dear!' said Mrs Warren. 'I *am* sorry!'

A burglary! Kate turned round to glance at Desmond, but Desmond was not looking at her. Desmond was not looking at anyone. He was staring darkly at his table, and his whole body had gone tense, and rigid.

'It was h-horrible!' Natasha sobbed. 'All our c-clothes, all messed about. My mum says she won't never get over it, not never!'

'When did this happen, Natasha?' said Mrs Warren.

'Yesterday afternoon,' said Ranjit. 'They got round the back and broke a window.'

'Was much taken?'

'The telly,' said Ranjit. 'And the hi-fi, and the video. They must have had a van to take it all away.'

'We know who done it,' said Florence.

'No we don't,' said Sarah. 'We don't really!'

'Yes we do, then,' said Florence. 'It was Desmond's dad.'

'I beg your pardon!' said Mrs Warren.

'Well, it was!' said Florence. 'Everybody's saying it.'

'How dare you repeat what everybody is saying!' said Mrs Warren, furiously. 'Who else in this class is spreading this rumour?'

'Not me,' said Matthew, with brazen disregard for the truth.

'Not me neither,' said Ashraf.

'It was the girls that started it,' said Curtis. 'I never believed it anyway.'

'*I* didn't believe it, Desmond,' said Daniel. 'I didn't, you know. Honestly!'

'Why say it, then?' said Mrs Warren in her most biting voice. 'And don't tell me you didn't, because it's only too clear that *something* has been upsetting Desmond very much, just lately. Frankly, now I know what it is I'm disgusted and disappointed with all of you. Especially the boys! What sort of friends are you to behave like that, I should like to know?'

Daniel squirmed. He was not a bad boy. None of them were bad boys, and they all liked Desmond really. It was just that a nice piece of juicy gossip was too good to pass over.

'It was only a bit of fun,' Curtis muttered.

'Well now, Curtis,' said Mrs Warren. 'Next time you feel like having a bit of fun, I suggest you take a moment to put yourself in the place of the person at whose expense you're having it!'

'Yes, Mrs Warren.'

'In fact, do it now. In your head, go on!'

'Yes, Mrs Warren.'

'And are you enjoying it, Curtis? Does it still seem like good fun?'

'No, Mrs Warren. . . . Sorry, Mrs Warren.'

'Yes – well, I'm not the person you've to apologize to, am I? In your shoes, Curtis – in your shoes, all of you boys – I should feel there was a wrong that needed to be put right. Do I make myself clear?'

'Yes, Mrs Warren.'

'Good. Right, Natasha, so the burglars took your telly. Perhaps you'll manage to get to bed at a reasonable time now.'

'They took something else as well,' said Sarah, with a vindictive glance at Natasha.

'*Yeah*!' Jennifer looked pointedly at Marie's blotched and swollen face.

'Well, come on,' said Mrs Warren. 'The suspense is killing us.'

'All right,' said Sarah. 'You know that bracelet you took away from Natasha that time.'

'I remember it,' said Mrs Warren.

'It wasn't Natasha's, it was Marie's. And Natasha wouldn't give it back.'

'I was only borrowing it for a few days,' Natasha proclaimed, indignantly.

'You should have give it back!' said Jennifer. 'She should have give it back, shouldn't she, Mrs Warren! Now the burglars got it, and Marie is going to get in trouble from her mum for lending it when she wasn't supposed to.'

'Neither a lender nor a borrower be!' said Mrs Warren.

'Natasha made her, though,' said Jennifer.

'Natasha is a bully,' said Sarah.

'I agree,' Kate whispered to Suzette.

'You do wrong things as well though, Kate,' said Suzette, reproachfully. 'You bunked off school, yesterday!'

Kate glanced anxiously in Mrs Warren's direction, but fortunately Mrs Warren did not appear to have heard.

'I *didn't* believe it, you know, Des,' said Daniel, on the way to the playground. 'About your dad. All the time, I didn't really believe it.'

'Nor I didn't neither,' said Ashraf.

'Nor me,' said Matthew. 'Not really.'

'Yes you did,' said Desmond. His eyes were on the ground, but his ears were straining for more of the same. If Curtis said it, he would let himself be convinced.

'*I* didn't believe it anyway,' said Curtis. 'It was only a bit of fun. *You* know it was only a bit of fun, don't you, Des!'

'You didn't ought to bunk off,' said Suzette to Kate, in the playground. 'You left me all by myself!'

'So?' said Kate. 'I nearly caught some burglars! Me and Desmond nearly caught them.' She was greatly excited; it was quite clear to her what had happened. While she and Desmond had been playing in the park, Scruffy and Bad News and the others had got together, and found a van, and done the burglary at Natasha's house. If she and Desmond had managed to stay on the trail, they could have caught the burglars red-handed!

'I didn't have a partner though, for going to the library,' said Suzette.

'So? What about all the times you stay away and *I* don't have a partner?'

'You didn't ought to bunk off, though.'

'If we hadn't of followed the wrong one,' said Kate, 'we would have caught the burglars!'

'I didn't have a partner for P.E. neither,' said Suzette.

'If we would have waited a bit longer at the dole place we would have caught them, most likely.'

'I didn't have a partner, though.'

'Me and Desmond will have to go on with our detecting now, won't we!' She was raring to go again. She couldn't wait.

126

'If you bunk off,' said Suzette, 'there's going to be *another* day I don't have a partner!'

Kate looked around the playground for Desmond, but today he was not alone. Today the boys were all competing with one another, to see who could be nicest to Desmond, and Desmond was right now happily tussling for a ball, with Curtis and Matthew and the rest. He was even laughing a bit, which was rare for Desmond.

They're making it up to him for being rotten, Kate thought, and saying all those things behind his back. Mrs Warren made them shamed, and good because they deserved it! It's all right anyway, we can meet after school. We can meet after school, and make some more plans. Not bunking off, of course, not that. Something though, there must be something! Now we know for certain who it is that's doing the burglaries, there must be something we can do! And anyway, it's going to be Saturday soon.

At home time, Kate hung about outside the school gate, waiting for Desmond to come out. She knew where he was; he was messing about with Curtis and the others, in the playground. Kate stepped back into the playground herself and did a few acrobatics, to attract his attention.

'What's the matter with Frog?' said Curtis.

Desmond glanced in her direction. Kate began mouthing and gesticulating grotesquely. Is she going to start on about doing detecting again, Desmond thought? She ought to know by now *that* doesn't work! We found out yesterday *that's* no good! Anyway, she ought to understand I want to be with the boys, now.

He felt a bit uncomfortable, a bit of a traitor, but Kate should understand that a boy wanted to be with boys. As long as they weren't saying things about his family. . . . As long as they could be trusted to go *on* not saying things, about his family.

'Do you get the feeling Kate's trying to say something?' Matthew sniggered.

'I get the feeling she flipped her lid again,' said Curtis.

Kate turned away with a sigh. It was disappointing that Desmond wouldn't look at her. Never mind, there was always tomorrow.

At home, Dawn was very sarcastic. 'Where you been today, then?'

'School, of course.'

'Oh? You sure you don't mean doing a burglary?'

'*Doing* a burglary?'

'You know. With your friend. Master Locke the burglar's son!'

Dawn was so pleased with this witticism, borrowed from Mum last night, that she said it again. And again, and again.

'I don't like you, Dawn,' said Kate. She hadn't meant to say that. She hadn't meant to think it, but somehow it slipped out.

'Don't be like that, Kate,' said Dad.

'I don't like her, though. What is there to like about her? She's lazy, and she's mean, and she's spiteful, and she tells tales. I don't know what Frank sees in her. And he is so nice, I think he ought to have a better wife than her!'

'*Kate*!' said Dad.

'I don't care what she says,' said Dawn, complacently. She spread her hands, in a gesture of disregard, and something flashed, on her wrist. Kate froze, staring at the flashing thing on Dawn's wrist.

'What you looking at?'

'Where did you get that bracelet?'

'My husband give it to me,' said Dawn, with pride. 'My husband that thinks a lot of me whatever you say!'

'Can I see it close?'

Dawn held out her arm. 'Why? You jealous?'

Kate shook her head. She wanted to shout, 'But that's Marie's bracelet!' Only something at the back of her mind told her not to, and she stopped herself just in time. In a minute, she thought. In a minute when I've had a chance to think!

'What's the matter?' said Dawn, uneasily.

'Nothing,' said Kate. She turned away and rummaged in her school bag to hide the shock in her face. 'I have to do my homework. Mrs Warren give us some homework to do.'

'Blimey, you're keen tonight,' said Dad. 'You only just now got home.'

'I want to get it finished with.' She spread her books on the dining table, and sat with her back to Dawn and Dad, chewing a piece of hair; and for a long time the thoughts wouldn't come at all.

Gradually, the fog in Kate's mind began to clear.

That *is* Marie's bracelet, she thought, it *is*. The big dark pieces joined together, and all those little gold bits, just the same! I don't understand – how could Frank gave Dawn Marie's bracelet? How could he come to have Marie's bracelet, to give it to Dawn?

I'm not going to think that thing I started to think. I'm not going to think it!

I know, I know, Frank bought the bracelet in the market! Like Marie's uncle bought it in the market

129

in the first place! The thief took the bracelet to the market, and Frank saw it there and bought it for Dawn. There! Now I don't have to think that other thing any more, so what about this maths Mrs Warren give us?

. . . There's something wrong with that idea about the market, though. That idea doesn't work properly, I think. . . . I know what is wrong, it's wrong because there wasn't time. The burglary at Natasha's house was yesterday, and that was Wednesday, and the market is only on Saturdays.

I'm *not* going to think that thing I was thinking! It's a terrible thing to think! Frank isn't a burglar, he can't be, and anyway he was at work yesterday, so that proves it.

I know, I know! The thief dropped the bracelet in the street, and Frank found it on his way home! . . . Only if he did that he should have taken it to the police station, not brought it home for Dawn. He *would* have taken it to the police station, I know he would! The thief couldn't have dropped the bracelet in the street, because Frank would have been honest and taken it to the police station.

So what else, what else? Come on, how else could it have happened?

. . . Of course! Why didn't I think of it before? Somebody gave it to him, that's what happened! Now all I have to do is ask Frank who gave him the bracelet, and we can go to the police together and tell the police who it was. Then we can give the bracelet back to Marie and everything will be all right.

It will be *more* than all right. It will be *better* than all right! I will be a detective after all. Hooray, I'm going to be a famous detective, and have my name in the paper! They won't tease me in school then, they will be jealous of me. . . . Not Dawn though, Dawn can't be in it. She can't be in it because she's a mean pig. Only me and Frank can be in it. 'Tra-la-la!' sang Kate, over Mrs Warren's maths.

'Shut up,' said Dawn. 'We're trying to watch telly.'

'You don't know what I know, though!'

'Who *wants* to know what you know?' said Dawn.

She must get Frank on his own, Kate thought. If she said it in front of Dawn, Dawn would want to be in it, and share the fun. But in a house like theirs, it wasn't easy to get anyone on their own. Kate listened, alert for the sound of a key in the lock. Sometimes Mum would be home first, and sometimes Frank.

Mum. In the kitchen preparing the meal.

Now! Now Frank was coming in! Kate leapt up from her chair, and ran to greet him in the hall.

'Frank!'

'Hello. You look excited!' *He* looked cold. *Blue* with cold. Perhaps he'd had to wait a long time for a bus.

'I want to ask you something.'

'Go on then, ask!'

'You know that bracelet, the one you give Dawn—'

'What about it?'

'Where did you get it from?'

'Where? . . . Why d'you want to know?'

'Tell me where you got it from, and I'll tell you why I want to know.' The eyes behind the crooked glasses sparkled with eagerness.

'. . . Bought it in the market, didn't I! Come on, let's get in the warm!'

'In the *market*?' The light went out of Kate's eyes. 'When?'

'When? . . . Last Saturday. . . . What's up?'

'Nothing.'

'You look upset about something.'

'No I'm not. I'm not upset about nothing. What is there to be upset about?' But her voice was stiff and tight, all of a sudden. Frank regarded her, his head on one side.

'Well, *I* don't know, do I? It's not me that's got the face as long as a piece of string! Come on, cheer up!'

'Why didn't you give the bracelet to Dawn on Saturday, if you had it then?'

'Why? . . . Because I forgot all about it, that's why. It was in my pocket, and I forgot all about it till last night. Satisfied?'

Kate gazed at Frank. She gazed, and gazed, as though she was seeing him for the very first time.

'What's the matter? What's all this fuss about a ordinary bracelet?'

But it wasn't an ordinary bracelet. It was an *old* bracelet, there was most likely only one in all the world. Didn't Frank know that? Didn't somebody tell him about old things yet?

'Do you want me to get *you* one, is that it?' She heard him as though from a distance, as though he had somehow gone far away. 'Tell you what – I'll go down the market again, day after tomorrow, and see if I can find a bracelet for you. That do? Happy now? . . . Can I get in the warm now?'

'Fra-a-ank!' called Dawn, from the sitting room.

'All right, Kate?' said Frank, jauntily but with just a touch of uneasiness.

'Yeah,' said Kate, in a small frozen voice.

Frank had lied! She could hardly believe it, but there it was, Frank had told her a lie! He said he got the bracelet in the market on Saturday. He said he had had it in his pocket ever since. But neither of those things could be true, because it was Marie's uncle who had bought it from the market, not Frank. And on Sunday Marie's uncle had given it to her for her birthday!

Kate dragged open the front door, and charged without her coat into the lamplit street. She had to be alone, and there was nowhere private in the house, and anyway she couldn't bear to be still. She hardly felt the cold as she ran, round and round the blocks, going nowhere in particular. She stopped in the end because she was winded; she stood on the pavement and took painful, gasping breaths. Then she began a stumbling walk, pleading inside as she went.

Don't let Frank be the burglar! Don't let Frank be the burglar! Oh, please, not that! Not that, *please*! The words went round and round in her head, until with a great effort she forced them to stop, so she could think.

. . . I wonder if there could be two bracelets after all! Could there just possibly be two bracelets, the same as each other? If there could be two bracelets, I would be happy for ever. If there could be two bracelets I would not ask for anything else in all my life. I don't *think* I would. Anyway, I would sleep in the sitting room for ever and ever. I would do that, I would, and not grumble about it neither. If only there could be two bracelets!

The trouble about that is, though, I can't believe there's more than one!

. . . I don't think Frank was very happy when

133

I asked him. I don't think he was very happy, and I don't think he knew what to say. I think he just tried to put me off when he said about going down the market to get a bracelet for me.

And he said he was just having a drink with a mate in that pub, but I think it could have been more than that, now. I don't think he usually goes to a pub in the middle of a work day, I don't *think* he does.

And he went off in a van, with the spotty one, like Desmond said. So that could be the van they put the telly in, and the hi-fi.

I don't think Frank went to work at all, yesterday, I think he just pretended. Perhaps he didn't go to work any of the days just lately. Perhaps he pretended to go to work, but really he went to do the burglaries. Oh, I don't like it, I don't like it! I don't want to be finding out these bad things, I don't!

. . . I know! I know how I can tell if Frank went to work today! When he goes to work he comes back with all paint round his finger nails. I shall go back to the house now, and look at Frank's hands, and see if there's any paint round the nails. Then I shall know for certain.

Once more, Kate began to run; but now there was a purpose, and a flickering hope. Kate clung to the hope and fed it as she ran. She even found room for a little bit of pride, that she thought out such a clever detecting idea.

At home, no one seemed to realize that Kate had been out. Only Frank looked up, as she came into the sitting room. 'All right, then? Happy?'

'Of course.'

She tried to say it naturally, but she couldn't bring herself to look at his face. She went close,

134

though, right up to where he was cuddling Dawn, and seated herself on the arm of the chair. 'Sit somewhere else!' said Dawn.

'Oh, plenty room!' said Frank, heartily, trying to coax a smile.

Kate's eyes were down. Frank felt her gaze, hard on the hand which was just now spread protectively over Dawn's lump. He shifted, not understanding the purpose of the gaze, but uneasy at the change in her manner.

'I have to finish my homework,' said Kate, suddenly jumping up.

'Oh, leave it!' said Frank. 'Leave it till after tea. Come and sit down again, come on!'

'No!' She couldn't look at him. Suddenly she couldn't even bear to be near him.

'What's up?' If you knew what to listen for, you could hear the anxiety behind the puzzlement in Frank's voice.

'What's it matter what's up?' said Dawn. 'She got the hump, that's all.'

'Don't be like that, Kate,' said Dad.

Kate collected her books, because Mum would want the table laid up for tea in a minute. She spread the books on the floor, and tried to focus on Mrs Warren's maths. But the figures danced and swam; the only thing Kate could see clearly was the picture in her mind's eye. The picture of Frank's clean pink hand, with its five clean pink nails – a hand which had most certainly not done any painting today.

9

Confusion and distress

Mrs Warren was on the rampage. Her judgement
soured by hunger, she had become overly aware of
the disgusting state of Class Seven's English books.
She had them in front of her now, and was going
through them, one by one.

'Curtis, is this your best work? Oh, how dare you
hand in anything less than your best! What's this
mess, Florence? The filthiest scribble I ever saw –
and you've managed to rub three great holes. . . .
Yes, well think with your head, not your rubber,
next time. . . . .There's a page missing from this
book, Ashraf. I beg your pardon – two pages!
Would you like to tell me where they are?'

Mrs Warren's voice grated on and on, floating
indistinctly somewhere above Kate's head. Kate
was not listening to Mrs Warren. Kate was totally
preoccupied with watching the thoughts that
churned round and round in her head, like the
clothes in the machine at the launderette. The same
thoughts had been going round all night, more or
less. Fresh bits got added, now and again, but
mostly it was the same thing over and over. And
over and over. And over and over and over. . . .

Frank was the burglar! He must be, it all fitted.
There was the bracelet, and seeing him in the pub
that time, and no paint round his nails last night.
There were the funny answers he had given when

136

she had asked him about the bracelet. There was the van that Desmond saw him going off in.

There was something else as well; Kate thought of it in the night. That policeman who came, the time Desmond threw the stone through the window – that policeman knew Frank from school. He said about somebody called Spotted Dick, that was a bad character. Or anyway, something like that. And Desmond said something about a 'spotty one' that was with Frank in the pub. Was that Spotted Dick? Frank said he finished with the old gang, but that didn't have to mean anything. Not now.

Frank was a liar, that's what he was – and all this time! Kate had loved him so much and all this time he was telling her lies, and telling Dawn lies, and telling Mum lies. What would they think, if they knew? What would they *do*?

Was it possible Dawn knew already?

Never! Dawn could never keep a secret like that, she wasn't brave enough. She would be scared all the time, and it would show. And she *wasn't* scared – just disagreeable. She wasn't a bit anxious when Frank was out, for instance, but if she knew he was out doing burglaries she would be all fidgety and jumpy. And she had no idea the bracelet was stolen; she was really proud of it, you could see! Oh, poor Dawn, poor Dawn, if she found out.

The offending English books had been returned. There was a new assignment. Everyone had been given just *one more chance* to produce acceptable work, and avoid the frightful but unspecified fate awaiting anyone unwise enough to fail. The task was an exercise in vocabulary. Mrs Warren had written some long words on the board, and you had to make up a sentence for each one, to show you knew what they meant. It was the sort of exercise Mrs Warren used to do when she was a little girl in primary school herself. Being on a diet seemed to make Mrs Warren rather fond of these exercises, though nobody else liked them very much. And this time, cruel Mrs Warren would not even help them with it. They could use their dictionaries, she said. Was there anyone who didn't know how to use a dictionary? There had better *not* be anyone who didn't know how to use a dictionary, because she had shown them often enough.

Suzette nudged Kate. 'I can't do it,' she whispered.

Kate pushed Suzette away.

'Help me, Kate,' Suzette begged. 'I can't do it.'

Kate put a piece of hair into her mouth and looked the other way.

'*Kate!*' Suzette insisted.

'What's the matter with you?' said Kate, loudly and roughly, yanking the wet strap of hair out of her mouth.

'Quiet, Kate!' said Mrs Warren.

'Tell her to leave me alone, then! She keeps bothering me!'

Suzette's pale eyes filled with tears.

'Get on with your work, both of you,' said Mrs Warren.

Kate chewed her hair again, and doodled on the page with her pencil. Beside her, Suzette sniffed occasionally, her chest heaving. She edged nearer, and sniffed over Kate's shoulder, blocking her view of the churning thoughts. 'Get away from me!' Kate hissed.

'But I can't *do* it!'

'Hard luck!'

'But I can't *do* it!'

Kate stamped, hard, on Suzette's foot.

Suzette shrieked. 'Whatever is the matter now?' said Mrs Warren – but her words were drowned by the sheer volume and intensity of Suzette's cries. 'Stop it!' said Mrs Warren, coming up to shake her. 'Just stop it!'

'She kicked me!' Suzette wailed, in sorrow and disbelief.

'She did *what*?'

'She hurt me!'

'*Kate!*'

'I'm sorry!' Really distressed by what she had done, Kate peered anxiously into Suzette's face. 'I'm ever so sorry, Suzette, I *am*!'

'So I should think!' said Mrs Warren. 'I can't imagine what's got into you today, Kate! What are you grinning about, Florence? . . . All right, Suzette, don't make a meal of it.'

Suzette wept on. Bored and irritated, Mrs Warren pretended not to see. Kate consigned the churning thoughts to the back of her mind, and concentrated on the business of cheering Suzette up. She pulled a few funny faces, which didn't work; then she got on the floor, and crawled round the table on all fours. Reaching the other side of Suzette, Kate pretended to be a dog, sitting up to beg. She panted, her tongue lolling. She took Suzette's hand and patted her own head with it. Suzette pulled away, but gave a watery giggle.

'*Work!*' said Mrs Warren, without looking.

'Kate's not doing no work,' said Florence. 'Actually, she's on the floor.'

'You ridiculous, unfunny little nuisance! Get up this minute!' Mrs Warren reached for Kate's book, saw the doodle and nothing else on the page, and her temper snapped. 'You haven't even started! You've had ten minutes, and you haven't even started. Well, *you know what I said!*'

'No,' said Kate. 'What did you say?'

'Tell her, Suzette.' Mrs Warren's voice was as grim as her face.

'You said we got one more chance,' said Suzette, fearfully.

'I don't know what we're supposed to do, though,' said Kate.

'Weren't you listening?'

'No.'

'I beg your pardon!'

'I just wasn't listening, that's all.'

'I see. You only listen when you feel like it, is that right?'

'Yes.'

There were a few subdued sniggers.

'Is there a joke, Curtis? Have I missed something amusing?'

'No, Mrs Warren.'

'Then take that silly smirk off your face. Kate, you had better come and work at my table. . . . Stop that blubbering, Suzette, you can have her back at playtime and welcome!'

Kate sat at Mrs Warren's table and tried to make sense of the words which seemed to be swimming about on the board. 'Put them in sentences!' Mrs Warren commanded. 'Go on, we've met all these words in our topic work this term. I didn't make them up out of my head.'

But the thoughts in Kate's head were going round like the laundry again, and the words on the board were getting all mixed up with the thoughts, and she couldn't seem to separate them out.

'Let me see what you've done,' said Mrs Warren, after another five minutes or so.

Reluctantly, Kate uncovered the still blank page. Mrs Warren looked at the book, and looked at Kate. 'Is something wrong?' she asked, in a softer tone. 'Are you worried about something?'

'No!' said Kate, in alarm.

'Something at home?'

'NO!' said Kate.

Some trouble with her mother, most likely, Mrs Warren thought: some argument. Mrs Warren had met Mrs Jackson and hadn't cared for her at all; a hard-faced woman, Mrs Warren thought, not much sympathy there. All right, if the child didn't want to talk about it, but it wouldn't do for her to brood. 'Come on, Kate,' said Mrs Warren. 'Best cure for worries is work!'

'I haven't got any worries,' Kate insisted.

'All right, you haven't got any worries. You were rude and spiteful this morning, which I have never known you to be before, ever. But this can't have been because of your worries, since you tell me you haven't got any.'

Mrs Warren wasn't being cross, for once; in fact there was a tiny smile, now, just twitching at the corners of her mouth. But to Kate, that smile was more threatening than any torrent of rage. That smile seemed to say that Mrs Warren could look right into her mind, and see the thoughts that were going round in her head. If Mrs Warren went on looking at her, and smiling like that, she would be able to see about Frank, and the bracelet, and Spotted Dick, and the van. All those terrible things that had to stay hidden, from everybody in the world.

'Stop looking at me!' Kate burst out.

'Ho, hum, don't be so conceited!' said Mrs Warren, still trying to jolly Kate out of her mood, 'Who wants to look at you?'

'You do! You're looking at me! I hate you when you look at me!'

'I *beg* your pardon!'

Kate's hands flew to her mouth. From behind the glasses, her horrified eyes begged Mrs Warren's forgiveness. A large tear rolled down each cheek.

Mrs Warren regarded the tears without speaking, for a moment. 'I shall pretend none of that happened!' she declared at last. 'We'll wipe it out, and start the day again. All right?'

Kate nodded, gratefully.

Watching all this, Desmond felt uncomfortable again. It had to be admitted, he hadn't been very nice to Kate yesterday, and now there was something wrong with her. She wasn't upset about *him*, was she? About yesterday? . . . No, it couldn't be that! It was something more. What?

. . . Anyway, the boys hadn't started saying things about his dad again, *yet*. He didn't trust them, though. They were all right today, but that didn't mean they were going to be all right again tomorrow, or the next day! Any time they could start again. Any time – till his dad was proved innocent, once and for all.

So *should* he get together with Kate, like she wanted, and try out some more detecting?

. . . Nah! Detecting was no good! Detecting was rubbish. Kids couldn't be detectives, not really!

. . . They had found out *something*, though,

hadn't they, him and Kate! When he stopped to think about it, Desmond saw they hadn't altogether wasted their time with that detecting. The trouble was, they couldn't follow up what they had found because they had to be in school, and they didn't have a car to go after people on motor bikes with, and they didn't have the things to take fingerprints with. . . . The police had those things, but he and Kate didn't have them. The police were pigs, of course. The police were the filth. . . . Nah, they couldn't go to the police, him and Kate! They couldn't do that. Could they . . . ? But the police would have to come into it in the end, there was no getting away from that.

'Kate!'

She was skipping with Suzette when he called her, and seemed curiously determined not to turn round. She ought to be pleased that he was taking notice of her again! Desmond went nearer, and yanked at her arm.

'What you want?'

'To talk to you, of course, what you think?'

'I'm busy.'

'This is important, though.'

'What is?'

'It's private!' said Desmond, glaring discouragingly at Suzette.

'Hurry up and tell me what it is, then,' said Kate, reluctantly following Desmond into a little space.

'What about we go to the police?' said Desmond.

'*What?*'

'What about we go to the police, and tell them what we know, about Scruffy and Bad News and them?'

'We don't know nothing!' said Kate, in alarm.

143

'Yes we do. We found out they got a gang. We could tell the police in case they didn't know about it. So the police can investigate, and find out they done the burglary.'

'I don't think they *did* do the burglary.'

Desmond was nonplussed. 'Yes they did, you *know* they did!'

'No I don't. Not really. That Bad News, he didn't do nothing wrong. He only just went to the dole place, to get his dole. I think we made a mistake.'

'He has been inside, you know!'

'So has your dad!'

It was a horrible thing to say. She was sorry as soon as she had said it. Desmond flinched, and turned sharply away.

During the afternoon, Kate was silent again, pre-occupied. With overcast face she stabbed away at her painting, and her thoughts.

What will happen about the bracelet, now? I can't give it back to Marie.

I wish I could tell someone! I know I can't, but I wish I could, because it is a very lonely thing to have it all inside me, all to myself. But I can't tell anybody, because I don't know anybody who will do.

Suzette is too stupid, and she would cry and tell her mum, I think. Desmond would be glad it's Frank and not his dad. Desmond would tell the police, I think, and I wouldn't blame him, because your own family has to come first. . . . I can't tell Dawn, because she will be too upset. . . . And Dad would be scared that Mr Duffy will throw us out of the house. . . . And I can't tell Mum, because you never know which way Mum is going to go.

And what about the bracelet?

I don't want Frank to go to prison, I don't!

I don't want Frank to know I found out about him. It would be embarrassing, and too hard to know what to say. Anyway, I don't want to talk to Frank at all just now. He has done a very bad thing; I don't want to talk to him, and I don't want to see him, and I don't want to be near him. I don't want Frank to go to prison, but I do want to be far away from him.

It's terrible about the bracelet, I can't bear to look at Marie!

And it's Saturday tomorrow, and Frank will be home all day, unless he goes to his mum's. He can't pretend to go to work and do a burglary really, because it's Saturday, so I suppose that's one good thing. And the same for Sunday. . . . But I'm dreading it, I'm dreading it because I will have to look at him, and talk to him, and I *can't*.

What shall I do? What shall I do?

At home time, Kate linked her arm in Suzette's and squeezed. 'Can I come home with you, say yes!'

'All right then.'

'I mean, can I come home with you to sleep?'

'I don't mind. . . . Where will you sleep, though?'

'In your bed, with you.'

'My bed's too small,' said Suzette, doubtfully.

'I don't take up much room.'

'. . . All right, then. Only I don't know if my mum will like it. She thinks you are a menace. She may not like you to sleep in my bed.'

'Will you ask her, though?'

'All right, I don't mind.'

145

                    *   *   *

'Where's Kate? said Frank, trying not to sound too
concerned.

'Stopping over Suzette's,' said Mum.

'Thank goodness!' said Dawn.

'Doesn't she see enough of Suzette in school?'
Frank was still slightly uneasy. He had come home
hoping to find Kate her old self again; it was a bit
disturbing not to find her at all.

'Oh, you know these girls!' said Dad. 'You know
how they like to gossip.'

'True facts,' said Frank, almost convinced.

Kate was crying. Her tears were not attracting
much attention because they were only a silent,
helpless trickle. 'What's the matter, Kate?' said Mrs
Warren, suddenly noticing.

Kate did not answer.

'Come on, Kate.'

'I can't do this maths.'

'Oh Kate, *really*! It's not like you to cry about
difficult work. . . . And anyway, this is easy!'

'I c-can't do it, though.'

'Oh, come on! No such word as can't!'

Desmond watched, and scowled, and struggled
with his pride – and made up his mind!

At home time, Kate ran all the way to the park,
by herself. Since she did not look round once, she
had no idea that Desmond was following her. It
was only when she sat on one of the swings, and
began to work herself half-heartedly backwards and
fowards, that she saw him coming towards her,
across the play area.

Desmond sat in the next swing. 'Hi!'

No reply.

                          146

'Do you know something?' said Desmond, not looking at Kate.

'What?'

'I think there's something wrong with you.'

'Do you?'

'Yes, I do.'

'You made a mistake. There isn't nothing wrong with me at all.'

'So why do you keep crying, then?'

'No reason.'

'And why aren't you going home?'

'No reason. . . . Why aren't you?'

'No reason.' Desmond twisted the chains of the swing round and round, then let them spin him as they unwound. 'Whee-ee-ee!' Looking carefully away again, he said: 'Come after you, didn't I? To find out what is wrong.'

'I didn't ask you to.'

'I know.'

'You should mind your own business.' She wanted to tell him to push off. She *ought* to tell him to push off really, because if he went on being nice, and not all snarly like usual, she might – Oh no, though, she mustn't! She mustn't let it out! Panic seized her. 'It's nothing to do with you!' she shouted at him. 'Why don't you leave me alone?'

Desmond was looking straight at her now, unmoved by the shouting. . . . 'I meant it, you know.'

'Meant what?'

'When I said I would look after you. I meant it.'

'Did you?'

'Yes, I did.'

'. . . Well, I don't want you to. Not any more.'

'All right, it's up to you!' Desmond got off the

swing and began to walk away, kicking at the turf with his down-at-heel trainers. He spun the round-about a couple of turns, then, slowly, carved a zig-zag path back to the swings. Once again he sat on the swing next to Kate, and presented her with the back of his head. 'Don't you like me any more, then? Don't you want to be in the Secret Two with me? I thought you did!'

'I didn't think you would like *me*. After that thing I said. About your dad.'

'Oh, that! I know you didn't mean it. You're not like that really; you're not like the others.'

'I'm sorry, anyway.'

'O.K., forget it!'

Kate was silent, her face downcast.

'. . . So what is the trouble?'

'I haven't *got* any trouble.'

'I think you have.'

He turned to look at her then, and there was so much concern on his face that the tears were in Kate's eyes, and rolling down her cheeks before she could stop them. She pushed up her glasses, to wipe them away.

'You *have*!' said Desmond. He averted his eyes from the tears and began to swing himself, slowly. Kate brushed her face with her sleeve and began to swing also. Side by side they swung, without speaking.

'. . . You can tell me, you know,' said Desmond, at last. 'I wouldn't tell anybody else. I wouldn't tell anybody else in the world.'

'I think you would,' said Kate.

'No I wouldn't! Who would I tell?'

'I'm not saying.'

Desmond frowned, struggling with the problem.

There was a sort of idea in his mind, but only sort of. '. . . Is it anything to do with the burglars?'

'Why do you think it's anything to do with that?'

'Is it, though?'

'I'm not saying.'

'It *is*, then!' He was looking at her again now, intently, seeking the truth from her face.

'I'm not saying! I'm not saying!' She knew she was going to, though, almost for certain; and she felt weak, and powerless, because she couldn't stop it happening.

Desmond pressed on. 'You said yesterday, you didn't think Scruffy and them done it.'

'I know.'

'But before, you thought they did.'

'I know.'

'Do you think it's somebody else, then?'

Silence.

'You do, don't you! You think it's somebody you know, you think it's somebody you like!'

'I'm not saying.'

'. . . It's not your dad, is it?'

'NO!'

Desmond considered. Suddenly, light dawned. 'I know, I know, it's that bloke we see in the pub! Your brother-in-law!'

'No, it's not.'

'I think it is, though.'

Kate burst into noisy sobs. 'Don't tell the police! *Please*, Desmond, don't tell the police!'

Desmond opened his mouth to say of course he would do no such thing, when the enormous implications of what Kate had just admitted hit him like a blow in the face, and he could only sit there, saying nothing at all.

149

'Desmond, please don't! Say you won't!'

She was a terrified, pitiful sight; he couldn't look at her. He turned his head away again, and muttered at the ground. 'Yeah – well . . . !'

'You're going to do it, aren't you! You're going to do it because of your dad, aren't you! You're going to do it to prove your dad is innocent. . . . Aren't you!'

Well, what did she expect! It was his chance, it was his big chance! It was the thing he wanted more than anything in the world, did she expect him to throw a chance like that away? Desmond swung himself silently, backwards and forwards, backwards and forwards, trying to still the turmoil inside him.

'I wish I never told you!' Kate wailed. 'I wish I never said nothing!'

'Yeah, well.'

'Yeah, well what?'

'Yeah, well . . . YOU DID!'

Kate hunched over, and buried her face in her arms. Desmond swung himself furiously for another minute, then abruptly got off the swing, and began to stumble away.

Kate did not call him back. Desmond began to run – faster, faster, out of the playground and across the grass of the park. He ran to the nearest tree and leaned against it, his arms tightly clasped around its trunk. He rubbed his face against the rough bark of the tree, and thought the feelings inside him would make him burst in a minute.

He turned to see what Kate was doing, and she was still there on the swing, slumped and despairing, with her arms across her face. What did she have to be like that for? What did she have to be all soft like that for?

Desmond took three deep, shuddering breaths, and began to walk slowly back.

'It's all right, I'm not going to tell.' The words were spoken roughly, without much kindness.

Kate did not move, did not even appear to have heard him.

'You deaf or something? I said I'm not going to tell!'

She looked up, then. 'Do you mean it?' she whispered.

'I said it, didn't I? I said it, what more do you want?'

'What about your dad, then?'

'Yeah, well . . . that's it, innit? Can't do nothing about it. You ain't supposed to grass on your mates, are you? Can't do nothing about it, that's how it is.' He kicked at the swing with savage brutality. 'Anyway, that's not all.'

'Isn't it?'

'No, it's not. The other thing is that I'm tough and you're soft. So it's up to me to put up with it. . . . Know what I mean?'

She gave him a tiny watery smile then, full of gratitude; and a great rush of compassion swamped the other feelings still seething and raging inside him. 'Yeah, well,' he muttered.

'What do we do now, then?'

'Nothing, I suppose. . . . Well, yes, yes, you got to tell me about it. You didn't tell me nothing about it, yet. Perhaps you made a mistake!' Now *there* was a hope! Perhaps she got it all wrong. Perhaps she went reading that rubbish book again, and got some wrong idea in her head, like before.

'All right, I'll tell you.'

She told him, while he dragged on the swing frame, and as the story unfolded, the brief hope faded.

'*Did* I make a mistake, Desmond?'

Desmond sighed, and kicked at the swing. 'Nah, I don't think so.'

'. . . So what now? You will have to tell me, Desmond, because I haven't got anybody else to help me, only you.'

He glared at her, again torn between pity and fierce resentment. What did it have to be that Frank for? What did it have to be somebody belonging to Kate for? Perhaps there was *still* some mistake. 'We better find out for certain.'

'How? she said, humbly. 'How, Desmond?'

'Find out if he really goes to work in the mornings, or if he just pretends.'

'How?'

'Follow him.'

'You mean bunk off again?'

'Yeah.'

'I can't! I can't. I got in trouble last time, my mum will *really* kill me if she catches me again!'

And Kate can't put up with that because she's soft, Desmond thought. It's like I thought before, *I* got to be the one. 'All right,' he said, 'I'll do it.'

'By yourself?'

'Yep.'

'You will bunk off by yourself, just for me?'

'No, *not* just for you! For me as well, what do you think? I want to know too, don't I? It's important for me as well, innit?'

'Oh, yeah – I see. For both of us.'

'Good. You got it. Tomorrow, then.'

His tone was terse, not very sympathetic, but at least he'd promised not to tell, Kate thought. And she couldn't blame him for the way he felt, she'd expected it after all. . . . Only please don't let him change his mind about telling, she thought. *Please* don't let him change his mind about that!

10

Certainty

'Does anyone know where Desmond is?' said Mrs Warren.

No one did, but Mrs Warren was not unduly concerned because there was a lot of 'flu going around, and a number of other empty seats that morning besides Desmond's.

Kate fidgeted, and tipped her chair backwards and forwards. 'Careful!' said Mrs Warren. 'You'll go over in a minute!'

Kate went over; her legs in the air, her knickers on display. Faridah and Nasreen averted their eyes from the unseemly spectacle, but the Super Six were greatly entertained. 'Do you intend to end up crippled for life?' Mrs Warren scolded Kate. 'With a broken back? Paralysed from the waist down? What an extraordinary sense of humour you have, Ranjit! Should we all come and laugh at *you* in a wheelchair?'

Suzette was away again. Kate spread her belongings over Suzette's chair and right across the table, pushing annoyingly at Faridah and Nasreen's things. She dropped her pencil, crawled on the floor to find it, and dropped it again, this time on purpose.

She was desperately, desperately nervous.

Desmond appeared, just before dinner time. 'Oh, *you've* managed to show up, have you?' said Mrs Warren.

'Dentist,' said Desmond.

'No note, of *course*,' said Mrs Warren.

Kate scanned Desmond's face anxiously, but his expression was closed, giving nothing away.

'Frog's gone all red,' said Florence.

'I think Frog fancies Desmond,' said Natasha.

'No I don't, then, what a silly thing to say!'

In his seat, Desmond scowled.

'Oo-oo-oh, *Kate*!' said Curtis, pointing and grinning.

'Leave off!' said Desmond, his face dark with anger. What did people want to start saying that for? It wasn't like that at all. Kate was not for fancying, Kate was for looking after.

He would have felt much the same about a dog if he had had one, or a rabbit.

In an agony of suspense, Kate tried to catch Desmond's eye, but Desmond was glaring at the table, and wouldn't look up. Ten minutes before it would be dinner time! Go, minutes, go, minutes, go!

But there was no chance of sitting next to Desmond at dinner, because the packed lunch people and the hot dinners people had their meals in separate rooms. And after dinner, of course, Desmond had to play a silly chasing game, with Curtis and the other boys. Jumping up and down herself to keep warm, Kate watched him charging in and out of the crowd, head down, deliberately not looking in her direction.

How could he! How could he not come and tell her what she was so desperate to know? It would only take a minute. Just a minute of his precious time!

Was there something he was *afraid* to tell her?

155

Had he decided to grass after all?

Had he *grassed* perhaps, already?

Waiting until hometime was like waiting for ever. Kate could hardly believe the waiting was over, when at last they were walking, side by side, down the road.

And now the time had come, she was *scared* to hear it – whatever it was that Desmond was going to tell her. She took deep breaths, and felt her heart going mad, inside her chest.

'Well, I followed him,' said Desmond. 'Like you said.'

'And . . . ?'

'He didn't go to work.'

'Oh.' That was it, then, all hope gone. Frank had made a great show about not being late for work this morning, but now the truth was out – he didn't go to work at all. And now what about the other fear?

'Why didn't you come and tell me in school?'

Desmond scowled. 'They're saying silly things about us, aren't they?'

'Is *that* all?' For a moment, the relief of it almost overshadowed the terrible news about Frank.

'What did you think it was?'

'I thought you might have grassed.'

'WHAT?' Desmond was outraged. The fact that yesterday he had considered doing just that made no difference to his sense of injury now. 'I told you – you don't grass on your mates!'

'I'm sorry.'

'And anyway, I said I wouldn't. Didn't I say I wouldn't?'

'I'm sorry, Desmond.'

Desmond kicked at the kerb. 'You don't trust me,

do you? he said, angrily. 'You trust everybody else. All the creeps and twisters like Frank, you trust them, but you don't trust me!'

'Yes, I do. I do trust you, Desmond. *I do trust you.*' Kate began to panic. Had she driven him away now? 'So tell me what happened. *Please* tell me what happened.'

Desmond kicked at the kerb again. 'He went down the canal,' he said grudgingly, at last. 'I followed him all along.'

'So where did he go after that?'

'Nowhere. Just the canal.'

'All by himself?'

'Yep.'

'All day?'

'Well, I don't know about that, do I! I wasn't there all day!'

'Why didn't you stay, to find out?'

'I was hungry, wasn't I? Had to come back for my dinner, what you think?' He hurled the words at her, his face a study in resentment.

'Of course you did, Desmond. Of *course* you had to come back for your dinner.' Her anxiety and distress were heartrending to watch. Once again, pity washed through Desmond, for the moment swallowing up all other feelings.

'It's bad, innit?' he said, in a softer tone.

'Yeah, it's bad. I suppose it's certain now, then, that Frank is the burglar. Is it certain, Desmond?'

'I don't see what else.'

They sat side by side on someone's wall. 'Desmond,' said Kate in a small voice. 'I don't know what to do.'

'Well, there isn't really anything you *can* do, is there?'

'There must be *something*.'

'Well, there isn't. Except you just have to go on like usual, and pretend you don't know nothing about it. That's the only thing you can do.' And who should know, Desmond thought bitterly, if *he* didn't?

Kate was silent, turning it over in her mind. 'But I can't!' she burst out suddenly. 'I can't pretend like that, I can't!'

'Well, you'll just have to, won't you?' After all, *he* had had to. *He* had had to turn a blind eye, often and often, to things it was better not to see.

The slow tears trickled down Kate's cheeks.

'Never mind, Kate! Never mind, eh?' Desmond groped for the right words. 'It's not so bad. I expect you'll get used to it.'

'No I won't, I'll never get used to that!'

They sat together on the wall. Desmond could think of nothing more to say, but he felt Kate fidgeting beside him, as though she was struggling with something in her mind. At last she spoke, in a stronger voice now.

'Desmond, how about if I have it out with him? With Frank. What about if I do that?'

Desmond shrugged.

'Do you think that could be a good idea?'

Desmond shrugged again. 'What is the point of it, though?'

'I could make him promise not to do any more wrong things.'

'What's the good for him to promise? He can just tell you some more lies.'

'*Desmond*. Don't say things like that!'

'There you go! Trusting the creep again!'

'Can't I just *try*, though?'

'. . . Nothing stopping you, I suppose.'

'It's what I'm going to do then. I'm going to do it tonight.' She sounded excited now, almost happy.

Desmond shrugged once more, and climbed off the wall. He kicked at the wall once or twice, then took a few scuffling steps down the road. There was no point in staying, there was nothing to stay for, now. Kate didn't need him any more – and it was worse than that. She wasn't just a person who didn't need him, she was a person who was standing in his way! She was the person who was stopping him from clearing his dad's name. Pity for Kate receded, as bitterness took its place.

'Where you going, Desmond?'

'Home.'

'Wait for me!' She jumped off the wall and hurried after him, prattling into his ear. 'That's what I'm going to do, Desmond. I'm going to say it out. I don't know what will happen, but anything's better than going on like this. Don't you think so, Desmond? Don't you think anything's better than going on like this?'

Desmond jerked away. Why didn't she just shut up?

It was all her fault he lost his chance, all her fault . . .

Kate did not notice that Desmond barely turned his head as she left him to go into her house.

Decision had given Kate new courage, and new strength. Eagerly, she had learned her little speech off by heart. She had practised it in her head, while pretending to be absorbed in a book. She had rehearsed it over and over, to be sure of not leaving anything out. And late that evening, after everyone else had gone to bed, she had her chance to say it. She was nervous now, her heart thumping, but she made herself go through with it.

'Frank!' He was standing at the television, about to turn it off, when Kate's head appeared round the corner of the sofa, to peer at him with blinking eyes.

'Cripes, you made me jump! You still awake, then?'

'I stayed awake on purpose.' Her voice sounded odd in her own ears – forced, and unnatural.

'Well anyway,' he said, with an uneasy little laugh, 'at least you're speaking to me again!'

Kate opened her mouth, and delivered her speech, all in one breath. 'I know where you got that bracelet from it belongs to a girl at my school and it was in a burglary and when I saw you in that pub the other day you were with Spotted Dick I think and you had a van like for putting the tellies in and I know you never went to work today because Desmond saw you down the canal. So that's how I know you're the burglar!'

Frank gaped at her. '*What*?' He tried to laugh, but the laugh didn't come out right.

'And you never had paint in your nails. Last week, you made out you come home from work, but you never had paint in your nails! And I don't think you could have washed it off, not really!' There! She had said it all! Now what was going to happen?

Frank sat down abruptly in the armchair. '*Kate*! You're imagining it all! You been reading too many books!'

'No, I haven't.

'I can explain all those things.'

'Go on, then, explain.'

'Well—'

'Go on, explain, explain!'

'All right, the paint for a start. I wasn't painting last week at all, I was hanging paper!'

'. . . Oh.' Suddenly there was a tiny trembling hope. Could the whole thing be one enormous mistake after all? That piece of detecting she had been so proud of, *that* had been a mistake. Perhaps they had worked the rest of it out wrong, her and Desmond.

'You see? It was all your imagination!'

'Not all of it, what about the rest?' *Please*, Frank, *please* show me the rest of it was just my silly imagination.

'Well . . .'

'Come on, I want to hear about the rest!'

'*Kate*! Give a bloke a chance to think!'

'I don't know why you have to think,' said Kate, bitter in her disappointment, as the little trembling hope dwindled. 'If you tell the truth you don't have to think.'

'All right, all right, this is the truth. I ain't got any work, have I? I ain't had any for three weeks, now! It's recession, innit! Most days I like make out I have got work, because I don't want Dawn to know. I don't want her to worry. With the baby and everything.'

Well, yes, *that* made sense. 'What about the bracelet?'

'I told you, I got it down the market.'

'You couldn't have.'

'I did . . . Have you told anybody else these crazy ideas?'

'Only Desmond.'

'Not your mum?'

'No. Don't you want me to?'

161

'Of course I don't.'

'Why not, if it's only my imagination?'

'Because . . .'

'Because what?'

'Because . . . .'

'You don't know what to say, do you?'

'You're not giving me a chance!'

'All right, I'll give you a chance. I'll give you a chance to prove that bracelet is not Marie's. Let me take it to school and ask her!'

'Nah . . . you don't want to do that!'

'Yes I do.'

'You'll only make yourself look silly.'

'I don't care. I can ask her to come here if you like, and look at it in this house. Shall I? Would you like me to?'

There was a long silence. Frank ran his fingers through his curls again and again, making them stand on end. He swallowed rapidly; even without her glasses, Kate could see the swallows rippling down his throat. His face was flushed, his eyes bright with real fear. He looked like a little boy, caught out doing something terribly naughty.

'Would you like me to?' said Kate, again. 'Ask Marie to come to this house? To see the bracelet?'

'. . . You know I wouldn't.'

'Why not?'

'. . . You know why.'

The little flickering hope finally died. 'Yes, I do.'

There was another long silence.

'You done all those other burglaries too, didn't you? Jacob's house. And the others in our road. You done them, didn't you?'

Silence again.

'You did, then.'

'It's no fun not having work, you know. It's not, you know, Kate. And Dawn likes nice things. And there's the baby.'

She hadn't thought of it like that. 'It's still wrong.'

'It's our secret, though, isn't it? Come on, Kate, I always stood up for you, didn't I? We was always good mates, wasn't we? You wouldn't give away our secret, would you?'

'No.'

'Would Desmond?'

'No.'

'Are you sure?'

'Yes, I'm sure, I'm sure.' Was there a tiny speck of doubt about that? Kate brushed the doubt away. 'I'm *sure*.'

'Well, there you are, then! There's no harm done after all. Phew! You had me scared for a bit!' He tried to smile, jauntily, but failed to make Kate smile back.

'I don't want you to do it any more, though,' she said, sternly. 'I don't like you to be a burglar, and I don't want you to do it any more.'

'Well, that's easy, because I wasn't going to anyway.'

'*Really?*' Kate's face lit up.

'Nah – I finished with all that.'

'Oh, Frank, I *am* glad!'

'Wasn't really me anyway, not really. You couldn't really say it was *me*.'

'Couldn't you?'

'Nah – just helping a friend out, wasn't I? He got the use of this van, see, but he didn't have a mate.'

'Spotted Dick?'

'Yeah – it was him done most of it. Getting rid

163

of the stuff and that. I mean, I just went with him on the job a few times. Like more of a lark than anything . . . Anyway, I finished with him now.'

'You said that before. You said you finished with all of them.'

'Yeah, well – ran into him the other day, didn't I? And one thing led to another. You know how it is.'

'Do I?'

'Oh, come on, Kate! You know how you get pulled into things! Your mates are doing it, so *you* do it. You just, like, forget yourself! *You* know how it is!'

'Like me bunking off with Desmond, that time.'

'That's right,' said Frank, eagerly. 'Like that.'

Kate was silent, chewing her hair.

'*Fra-a-ank!*' called Dawn, from the bedroom.

'Frank?' said Kate.

'What?'

'Did you? . . . You know! . . . Today?'

'Nah . . . . All right, I was going to meet him, but he never showed up. And that's the truth, on my mum's life!'

'And tomorrow you will tell Dawn there isn't no work, and you will go to the dole place.'

Frank swallowed and looked away.

'You will, won't you, Frank? Or you can look for another job.'

'Yeah, all right.'

'You promise?'

'*Fra-a-a-ank!*' called Dawn, from the bedroom.

'Coming!' he called.

'You promise?' said Kate, again.

'All right, all right!' He must agree with whatever she said. She could open her mouth if he didn't,

164

and then what? Just get past this tricky bit now! Keep her happy! Keep her happy!

'FRA-A-A-ANK!' Dawn was at the end of her patience.

'I shall have to go.'

'All right, then.'

'You won't tell anyone!'

'No.'

'You sure?'

'I won't tell anyone, I said!'

'It can be our secret, eh?'

'All right.'

'It'll be great having a secret, it'll be good fun!' He was trying to be jaunty again. 'I mean, you and me was always best mates, so now we got a secret together it's really good, innit!'

'Yeah,' said Kate, doubtfully.

'FRA-A-A-ANK! ARE YOU COMING TO BED OR WHAT?'

'All right, then, Kate?'

'Yeah, all right.'

Under the duvet, with the pink and yellow flowers, Kate curled into a tight little ball. I *did* it, she thought triumphantly. I *did* it. I was scared at first, but it wasn't so bad in the end. And the main thing is, Frank is not going to do any more burglaries.

And I'm not going to tell on him, I'm not! I don't think it will be fun having the secret, like he said. I don't like secrets, actually. But anyhow I'm not going to tell on him.

I wish my mind would not go so fast, inside my head.

I still like Frank, I do! It wasn't his fault really, it was Spotted Dick's fault. And anyway, Frank didn't do it for himself, he did it for Dawn and the baby. And he said that nice thing about we're best mates.

I wish I could get to sleep . . . .

Oh, I just thought of something! I just thought of something terrible! The police! The police didn't find out about Frank yet, but suppose they do? They are doing their detecting about the burglaries, they must be! Going to the houses, and taking fingerprints and things! Suppose they find Frank's fingerprints! Suppose they come to the house, and ask him questions? Suppose they ask *me* questions!

Oh no, oh no, don't let that happen! I shall get all muddled up, and it will be too much for me. I'm scared, I'm scared!

I don't think I'm ever going to get to sleep tonight.

I know what I'm going to do, I'm going to forget about the police coming. I'm going to make myself think it will be all right, and they won't find out. Probably they won't, anyway. No, I'm *sure* they won't. Probably God won't let the police catch Frank now he has decided to go straight. He will give him one more chance. Probably.

So that's all right!

. . . I just thought of something else, only I wish I didn't. Suppose Frank doesn't keep his promise!

He told a lie, he could tell another, like Desmond said. He told a lot of lies, he could tell a lot more, how would I know? I wish Desmond never said that thing.

I can't bear it if Frank is still telling me lies.

I'm going to believe Frank, I *am*.

. . . I *love* Frank.

166

* * *

'It's all right now, Desmond,' said Kate with a shining face. 'Frank's going to go straight, he *promised*.'

'. . . Good.'

'He meant it, you know. He did mean it!'

'. . . Good.'

'Is that all you can say?'

Desmond shrugged. 'What more do you want?'

'You two made it up, then?' said Mum.

'Make it up? There wasn't nothing to make up, was there, Kate? We was always best mates, wasn't we!'

'Always,' said Kate, beaming.

'Oh, pardon my mistake, I thought you fell out.'

'Well we didn't,' said Kate. 'And we aren't going to, are we, Frank?'

'Hi, Desmond,' said Kate.

'Oh, it's you.' His voice was grudging, surly.

'You don't seem very friendly to me, just lately.'

'Don't I?'

'Did I do something wrong?'

'Nope.'

'So what is it all about?'

'Nothing.'

Kate gave up.

'Got you a little something today, Kate,' said Frank.

'Did you?' Kate's cheeks were pink with pleasure. 'What?'

It was a cheap trick puzzle, on a card with a plastic cover. 'It's a lovely present!' Kate declared.

'What you go buying that rubbish for?' said Dawn. 'We can't afford it, till you get another job.'

'Yeah.' Frank sighed. The days were going by, and they were long and empty. No hope from the old firm, the old firm was about to go bust. And what hope of a job elsewhere?

'Never mind,' Kate beamed at him. 'You haven't got much money, but you have got *us*!'

'What are you going to call the baby? said Kate.

'Jason,' said Dawn. 'Or Gemma.'

'Kate's a nice name,' said Frank.

'Ugh!' said Dawn, in disgust.

'Would you *really* call the baby my name, Frank?' said Kate thrilled.

'Would you like that?'

'Oh, *yes*.'

'I think you've gone mad,' said Dawn.

'Isn't it good?' said Kate. 'There doesn't seem to be any more burglaries round here, just now.'

'Oh?' said Mum. 'I thought you wanted the burglars to be getting on with it, so you could catch them!'

'Oh, no!' said Kate. 'I gone right off *that* idea.'

Way down the road, Desmond trudged to school. Kate knew Desmond was behind her, but she didn't wait for him to catch up. Desmond might say things she didn't want to hear. Or he might hint at things she didn't want to think about. And anyway, he seemed to have gone off her, just now. That was all right, Kate decided, because she'd gone off him.

As long as he kept his promise not to tell.

Oh, but he would, he would! He promised, and anyway you don't grass on your mates, he said.

Even if they aren't very much your mates any more?

I'm not going to think about that, Kate thought. It's too much for me, I'm not going to think about it!

11

Truth will out!

Jacob was sitting on the wall outside his house. 'What you sitting there for, Jacob?' said Kate.

'Lost me key, innit!' said Jacob, gloomily.

'Your mum's going to go mad!'

'I know.'

Kate sat on the wall with Jacob, to keep him company. There was a little gossiping crowd across the road. 'I think Bruce is dead,' said Jacob.

'*What?*'

'Them across the road said he's dead. Burglars hit him over the head. They come when Mrs Harris was up the shops.'

'*What?*'

'Those burglars come again. They got in her house and they hit poor old Bruce on the head.'

'I don't believe it!'

'Them over there said they done it to keep him quiet, but I think they're just cruel.'

'I don't believe it!' said Kate, again. 'I don't believe it, I don't!' Stunned with shock, and grief, Kate turned away and stumbled down the road.

'Come back!' Jacob called after her; but Kate had heard enough. She put her fingers in her ears and began to run.

'Kate!' Jacob called. 'Come back a minute!'

He wanted to tell her he knew something else. He wanted to tell her that the police had been, and that them over the road said the police had a *very good idea* who the burglar was.

In the house, Dawn and Dad were watching television, as usual. Frank was not at home. There was strident laughter from the television's studio audience. 'Do we have to have that noise all the time?' Kate's voice was rough; she didn't recognize her own voice. Dawn stared at her.

'What's up with you, then?'

'Nothing. Just you can't think about nothing except telly, telly, telly! Nothing but telly, all day long!'

'Don't be like that, Kate,' said Dad.

Kate burst into tears. She sat at the dining table, and the sobs tore through her. 'If there's something really wrong, you better tell us what it is,' said Dawn.

The desperate crying went on and on. Even Dad, wrapped from morning till night in his shroud of self-pity, was concerned. 'Cheer up, Kate, it can't be that bad!'

'It is.'

'What is?'

'It's the w-worst thing I could th-think!'

'You fell out with Suzette?' Dad suggested. Dad's imagination never did stretch very far.

Kate's head, resting on her arms, rubbed itself from side to side.

'You haven't been *suspended*?' Dawn sounded as though she mighty actually enjoy a little titbit like that.

'No!'

'So what, then?'

Kate lifted her head. The glasses hung from one

171

ear, and her nose was running. 'You look disgusting!' said Dawn.

Suddenly Dad was alarmed. This trouble – was it something Mr Duffy could take exception to? Was it something that could get them all turned out?

Kate's head dropped on to her arms again. 'Bruce is dead.' Dad seized the muffled words with relief. Not trouble for the family, only somebody he didn't know, dead!

'Who's Bruce?' said Dawn, not caring very much. 'Mrs Harris's d-dog.'

'All that fuss about a *dog*?' said Dawn scornfully.

'He was a lovely dog, though! He was a lovely dog!'

'Oh, shut up about your lovely dog! We're sick of hearing about your lovely dog!'

'Shut up, yourself!'

'Come on, girls!' said Dad.

'There's something the matter with her, though,' said Dawn. 'There must be. She must have a screw loose. Crying and bawling about a *dog*!'

'You don't know nothing about it!' Kate burst out.

'And I don't want to.'

'You don't know nothing about it! You don't know nothing about it!' Beside herself now, Kate screamed the words.

Grinning, Dawn heaved herself and her lump out of the chair, and turned the television up full blast.

'I hate you!'

'Don't be like that, Kate,' said Dad, his voice quite drowned by the sound of the television.

Dawn grinned again, and cupped her hand to her ear. 'What was that?' she mocked.

Inside Kate, something snapped. 'I hate you, and I hate Frank! I wish I never met neither of you!'

'This is giving me a headache,' Dad complained – and he turned the television off.

'Oh, you hate Frank now!' Dawn jeered. 'That makes a change from being all over him! What's Frank done, then?'

'Wouldn't you like to know!' Kate screamed at her.

'Yes, I would,' said Dawn, suddenly uneasy.

'Well bad luck! Because I'm not going to tell you.'

'You're making it up!'

'No, I'm not.'

'You're making it up because you're jealous that Frank is my husband, but he's only your brother-in-law.'

'Huh!' said Kate, bitterly.

'You're jealous, jealous, jealous!' said Dawn, with a smug little laugh.

The injustice stabbed and seared. 'Jealous? What is there to be jealous of? I don't want nothing to do with somebody that kills other people's dogs—' Kate stopped suddenly. What had she said, what had she said?

'*What* did you say?'

'You heard.'

'*Kate!*' said Dad.

'I didn't mean it,' said Kate.

'Yes you did!'

'I made it up because I was jealous, like you said.'

'I don't believe you.'

'I think we should forget all about it,' said Dad.

'I can't forget that, though, can I!' said Dawn.

'What a horrible thing to say! I don't know *what* to think now. What am I supposed to think?'

'Think what you like.'

'You nasty, spiteful little cow! You wait till our mum comes home! You wait till I tell her what lies you been saying!'

'It's not lies.'

'You just now said it is.'

'Well, it's not! It's not!' Kate was screaming again. She knew she was contradicting herself. There were warning bells, somewhere in the back of her mind, telling her to stop. But she couldn't, she couldn't! Still in shock, the tide of rage and grief was sweeping her headlong; she must go with it, whether she wanted to or not.

'I'll show you if it's lies, I'll show you, I'll show you!'

'Come on, then.'

'All right, I will. You tell me where Frank is now. You just tell me!'

'*I* dunno,' said Dawn.

'Yes you do, Dawnie,' said Dad. 'He went to sign on.'

'That was this morning,' Dawn admitted. 'I dunno where he is now. I was wondering, actually.'

'Well there you are,' said Kate. 'That proves it.'

'Probably up the Job Centre,' said Dad hopefully. 'Or round his mum's.'

'Proves what?' Dawn persisted. 'Come on, Kate, you can't stop now.'

'Don't worry, I'm not going to stop! I know why Frank didn't come home. He didn't come home because he was doing a burglary, so there! He done a load of burglaries before, and now he done another one!'

'You're mad!'

'No, I'm not! I'm not mad! You're always saying I'm mad. But I know more about Frank than you do, because he told me!'

'He never! He wouldn't!'

'He did, then, because I found it out. See? Clever-clogs Dawn, that's always saying I'm mad!'

Dawn was silent. Dad looked totally stricken. For a few moments, Kate felt a sort of bitter exultation. *That* showed them! *That* made them think!

Then Dawn got up and turned the television back on. The studio audience was still cackling away. 'So?' said Kate.

Dad said nothing.

'So what?' said Dawn.

'Weren't you listening?'

'It's a load of rubbish. I don't believe a word of it.'

'Yes, you do.'

'I don't. Anyway, I'm not going to.'

'You better! You better believe it!'

'Shut up,' said Dawn. 'I'm trying to watch telly.'

Dad said nothing.

Kate's head felt light and swimmy now, with the full realization of what she had done. She had told! She had given away Frank's secret! The thought filled her mind, blocking out everything else, even her grief for Bruce.

'Where's that Frank got to?' said Dad, after a long time.

'Are we watching telly, or not?' said Dawn.

Mum came in, at last.

'Kate been telling lies,' said Dawn.

'Wicked ones!' said Dad.

'Kate don't tell lies,' said Mum. 'It's a well

175

known fact that Kate don't tell lies. So what is all this about?'

'You tell her!' said Dawn. 'Go on, Kate, you just tell Mum what you said!'

Silence.

'All right, please yourself,' said Mum.

'Shall I tell it, then?' Dawn appealed to Dad.

'It's only a load of old codswallop,' Dad insisted.

'Yeah, but she didn't ought to have said it.'

'I got something better to do than stand here listening to you two arguing!' said Mum.

'All right, don't go, don't go!' said Dawn. 'I'll tell you! Kate reckons Frank's a burglar!'

Mum shrieked with laughter.

'I thought you'd laugh!' said Dawn, relieved. 'She must be mad, mustn't she!'

'Or wicked,' said Dad.

'Come on, Kate,' said Mum, still grinning. 'What's this daft idea you got in your head?'

They were laughing at her again, and it was nothing to laugh at, nothing! 'It's not daft,' she shouted. 'It's the truth!'

'All right,' said Mum, putting her hands over her ears. 'Spare a thought for our eardrums!'

'It's the truth,' said Kate, in a small still voice.

'What is?' said Mum, sharply. She was not laughing now. 'What's the truth, Kate?'

'You ain't going to *believe* her, are you?' said Dawn.

'I don't know yet,' said Mum.

'It's a load of old codswallop,' said Dad.

'Shut up, you!' said Mum. 'Kate, I'm waiting.'

She was going to have to tell on Frank, again. There was no choice now, she was going to have to do it. And he *did* deserve it, he *did*. For killing Bruce, and breaking his promise, he deserved to have her tell.

'I know it's true because he told me,' said Kate.

'Told you what?'

'Don't listen to her,' said Dad.

'Shut up, you! Told you what, Kate?'

'He done all the burglaries. All the burglaries in this road. Him and a old mate from school. He told me.'

Mum's eyes went hard.

'Is that why you fell out? Week before last, is that why you fell out?'

'Yeah.'

'She's making it all up,' said Dawn, desperately. 'She's making it all up because she's jealous.'

'If anybody's jealous it's you!' Mum spat at her. 'Just because he shows her a bit of kindness now and again! . . . Why did he tell you, Kate? Whatever made him tell *you*?'

'I found him out. It was because of the bracelet. That one Dawn's wearing now. It belongs to Marie, in my class. And there was other things . . . Like he only pretended to go to work. And I found it out. Me and Desmond found it out. And then he admitted it all. And he said to keep it a secret.'

'She's off her trolley!' said Dawn.

'. . . She's telling the truth,' said Mum.

There was a great silence in the room. Bewildered and dismayed, Dawn and Dad sat like waxworks. Mum's face was grim. 'I never did trust that boy,' she said at last, through tight lips.

'You did, you did! You liked him! You always said you liked him, you did!'

'I didn't trust him, though. He got shifty eyes, I always thought so.'

'You never said that!'

'Are you arguing with me?'

'You did use to like him, though,' said Dawn, piteously.

'Well, I never wanted you to get married. You was too young, for one thing. Him as well by his ways. You was like a couple of kids, playing at being grown up.'

'We're going to get throwed out now,' said Dad. 'For certain.'

'I think I'm having a dream,' said Dawn. 'I shall wake up in a minute.'

'You've woke up now!' said Mum. 'And if you don't like what you've woke up to, don't try saying I didn't warn you!'

'We're going to get throwed out,' said Dad.

'Shut up, you!' said Mum.

She went into the kitchen then, and began banging about, making the meal. In the sitting room no one spoke, and no one looked at anyone else. What would happen when Frank came home? That was up to Mum, of course. Mum made all the decisions in their house, and you never knew which way Mum was going to go.

They sat round the table in silence, and played with their food. They glanced at Mum from under lowered lids, and saw that her eyes were like granite, and there was a tiny red patch on each sallow cheek. At the sound of Frank's key in the lock, Dad went ashen, and slumped in his chair. Now! Now the great fear of his life was about to come to pass!

Kate felt funny. There was no other word for it, she felt *funny*. She felt as though the room around her had somehow spread out, so the furniture and the walls were a long way away. The people in the room were a long way away, as well. She was all by herself, in a big empty space, a big *unreal* space – waiting for something quite unreal to happen.

Frank came in, staggering and trying to look jaunty. His hair was messed, his jacket was torn, and he smelled strongly of beer, which was unusual for Frank. There was a bruise on his forehead, and what looked like blood on his sleeve. Sickened, Kate turned away.

'Where you been?' said Dawn, faintly.

'Nowhere. Jus' out.' His speech was slightly slurred, and he had to clear his throat to get the words out.

'You're drunk!' Dawn accused him.

'True facts.' He giggled. 'Drunk and disorderly.'

'All right,' said Mum. 'GET!'

'What?' Frank gaped at her.

'GET!' said Mum, again. 'Get your things packed, and get out this house, and don't never come back again!'

'No!' Dawn protested.

'Whafor?' said Frank, his fogged mind trying to grasp what was happening now. 'What have I got to go for?'

'You know!'

Frank's legs gave way, and he sat down heavily on the sofa. 'Come on, Ma – it was only a couple of pints!'

'And the rest! But I'm not talking about the disgusting state of you, I'm talking about something else.'

'What?'

Mum's stare was unnerving. Frank's eyes slid away from her gaze.

'What?' he said again, in a shaky voice.

'Ask Kate!'

'What about?'

'You know!'

Frank looked at Kate, and at Mum, and back at Kate once more. He took a breath, and let it out again. He took another one. He looked really frightened now.

'Only because you went and killed Bruce! Only because of that!'

'*What?*'

'Only a dog,' said Dawn.

'He was a darling dog,' said Kate. 'And I wouldn't have told on you else, you know I —' She broke off, and began chewing frantically on a piece of hair.

'Just a minute, just a minute – I never killed no dog!'

'Spotted Dick, then, but you helped! You burglared Mrs Harris's house and you went and killed her dog to keep him quiet.'

'No! Kate, you can't think I'd do something like that! You can't think that, Kate!' He gazed at her, his eyes full of reproach. 'Anyway,' he blundered on, 'you don't pick a house with a dog to go in. It ain't worth the risk!'

'You *have* been doing your homework!' said Mum.

'I dunno what you're all on about, I don't! I been in the pub, that's all.'

'We can see *that*,' said Dad, recovering enough to join in.

'Ain't I allowed?'

'Depends who you was with.'

'I wasn't with nobody. I went on my own, I can prove it.'

'What about before?' said Mum. 'Come on – before the pub, who was you with then?'

'Nobody!'

'How we suppose to believe that?' said Mum.

'You tell lies,' said Kate. 'You tell lies all the time. I don't believe anything you say, any more!'

'I never done no job today, I never!' said Frank. 'On my mum's life, I swear it!'

'What's the use to swear,' said Kate, 'when you tell so many lies?'

Frank was silent. He shifted from side to side on his seat. Kate had told. Mum knew the whole story. He was done for now, whatever he said.

'So that wraps that up,' said Mum.

Frank turned desperate eyes in her direction. 'I don't know nothing about no dog. I never done no job today, I don't know nothing about no dog!'

'How many *have* you done, then? Four? five? . . . Come on, how many?'

Frank shrugged.

'All right, don't tell me. Same difference. Get your things packed like I said, and get out! We're not having no criminals in this house. This is a respectable family, this is. We're not having no rubbish out of the gutter bringing disgrace on *this* family! So you take yourself off, and sharp about it!'

'No-o-o!' wailed Dawn. 'And don't say things like that about Frank!'

'Yes!' said Mum.

'You can't throw him out, you can't! He's my husband, and what about the baby? You can't throw him out!'

'Watch me!' said Mum.

Dawn began to cry; great gulping, hysterical sobs. Mum slapped her face, hard.

'Don't hit my wife!'

Mum slapped Dawn again.

Frank lurched to his feet and went to get between Dawn and Mum. He put his arms round Dawn, and nuzzled her.

'Go on!' said Mum. 'I said to get out!'

'That's right,' said Dad. 'She said to get out.'

Frank hugged Dawn closer. 'You coming with me, then?'

'You stop where you are, Madam!' said Mum, sharply.

'She's my wife,' said Frank.

'She's useless, and you know it! You got enough problems without her going to pieces all over you!'

'Dawn?' Frank pleaded, not quite so ardently.

'Where?' said Dawn. 'Where we going to go?'

'I dunno for the minute. I'll find somewhere.'

There was a fresh outburst of crying. 'I don't know what to do! I don't know what to do! Somebody make all this go away! Make it like it was before!'

'See what I mean?' said Mum, contemptuously.

Frank's arms dropped to his sides, and he stood back. He took one or two deep breaths, made a move towards Dawn again, then looked at her lump and looked away again. 'Nah,' he muttered. 'Best stay with your mum.'

She clutched at him. 'Frank! Don't go!'

'I got to, Dawn, I got to!' His voice was rising in pitch.

'No, don't! Don't!'

'I got to, though!' His voice had risen to a squeak. 'I go to, haven't I!'

182

Oh God, he was in a mess! The worst mess he ever was in, in his life. With the alcohol clearing from his brain he began to grasp just how terrible the mess was. It wasn't a lark any more, it was serious trouble. And there was no refuge for him here, that much was pitilessly clear. Escape! Escape from the mess! Never mind anything else now, just escape!

'But where you going? Where you going?'

'Don't tell us,' said Mum. 'We don't want to know.'

'I wasn't going to,' said Frank. 'I'm not a imbecile.'

'That's a matter of opinion,' said Mum.

'*I* want to know!' said Dawn. 'I want to know where Frank's going.'

Mum laughed, harshly. 'Why? So you can give it away to Old Bill, when they come asking questions? They'd get it out of you in no time, and don't think they wouldn't!'

A look of panic flashed across Frank's face. Dawn began to shriek. Frank tried to take a step towards the door, but Dawn gripped him fiercely. He tried to unclasp her hands, but she cried all the louder, and wouldn't let go. The two of them began a grotesque sort of dance, as Frank unwillingly dragged the clinging Dawn into the passage and down to their bedroom.

It was the most distressing thing Kate had ever witnessed in her life.

'Do you reckon she'll go?' said Dad.

'Not her!' said Mum. 'Anyway, he wouldn't take her. He don't want her hanging round his neck after what I said. You can see he's not bothered about her right now. He's too scared for his own skin.'

Kate was crying wretchedly. 'I think I didn't ought to have told.'

'Yes you did,' said Mum.

'Well, anyway, I think you didn't ought to have made Frank go. I think you didn't ought to have done that.'

'Oh? We running a hostel for criminals, then?'

'Frank is our family!'

'Not any more.'

'But he is, he is!'

'He's a thieving little scumbag! Anyway, if you ask me, at this moment he can't get out of the house fast enough!'

'Because he's scared of you,' said Kate.

'So I should hope!' said Mum. 'But it ain't only that. Something's happened he's not letting on, you mark my words!'

'What?'

'I reckon the Old Bill's on to him, and I reckon he knows it. He's scared out of his pants. He was scared when he come in, I could smell it on him with the beer. Which he got outside of because he was scared in the first place. Let him go, and good riddance!'

'We're all going to get throwed out, anyway,' said Dad, 'when they come here asking their questions.'

'Oh, put another record on!' said Mum.

12

A nasty surprise

They were gossiping again, in the playground. Jacob had brought the news, about the new burglary in Wessex Road, and once more the children were convinced it must be Desmond's dad who had done it. Particularly as the police had such a good idea on the subject!

Desmond stood apart, glaring at the ground and trembling with rage. I *knew* they'd start saying that again, he thought, I just *knew* it! And the worst of it is, the worst of it is, I know who *really* done that burglary, probably, and I can't tell. Can I?

I think I'm going to explode in a minute, I think I'm going to go off bang! It's not fair I'm not allowed to tell, it's just not fair. And there's Kate Jackson, and she knows who done that burglary as well, she must do. And she's all by herself, and she looks as miserable as anything, and it serves her right to be miserable, because it's her fault me and my dad got to put up with all this rubbish!

It won't be that Frank the police got their idea about, oh no! It'll be my dad again, I bet!

Suppose I told after all? I know you're not supposed to grass on your mates, and I never did. What about grassing on somebody that *used* to be your mate though, what about that?

In class, the gossiping stopped, even the whispers. No one wanted Mrs Warren to catch them doing it, and tell them off like last time. Which she would surely do, even though she was in an amazingly good mood this morning.

Mrs Warren was in a good mood, largely because this morning her tummy was comfortably full of toast and marmalade. She had starved herself now for four weeks (not counting the occasional cheat), and how much thinner was she? A miserable five pounds thinner, that's all! Each time she went on a diet it was harder to lose the weight, it seemed. How unfair! What an unfair world we live in, Mrs Warren thought.

All right, Mrs Warren told the unfair world, you needn't think you're going to get the better of *me*! If I can't be thin and beautiful, I'll be *fat* and beautiful . . . so there!

For four weeks, Mrs Warren had taken out her sufferings on Class Seven, and lessons had been dull and formal. She herself was sick of the stale old stuff. 'We'll do something different today,' she told them all. 'Something fresh. We'll start a class newspaper, how about that? A real one. We'll put everything on the computer, and make a copy for every class. What do you say?'

'Can we write about Natasha's burglary?' said Ranjit.

'Well, yes, I suppose so. If you really want to.'

'I know somebody else that's house got burgled.'

'I know somebody else, as well.'

'Did you hear about the one yesterday, Mrs Warren? The one in Wessex Road?'

'That's enough,' said Mrs Warren. 'A gold star for the best work *not* about burglaries.'

Staring into space, Kate was only vaguely aware of the voices around her. Her body was in the classroom, but her real self was at home with Dawn.

186

Dawn who had cried and cried last night – bitterly and inconsolably, because Frank had gone, and she didn't know if she would ever see him again. And Kate wanted to cry like Dawn; she wanted to, only somehow she couldn't, because she had cried so much already the tears were all dried up.

'Is something wrong, Kate?' said Mrs Warren.

'NO!'

'I beg your pardon, I thought there might have been. What is it, then, are you stuck for ideas?'

'. . . What?'

Mrs Warren looked at Kate thoughtfully. 'I'll give you till dinner time to buck up. Just until dinner time.'

Why doesn't Mrs Warren tell Kate off for being lazy, thought Desmond. Mrs Warren is too soft to Kate! Why should Kate get away with it, just because she puts on that miserable face?

'Frog has turned into a zombie,' said Ashraf, whispering into Desmond's ear. Desmond jerked away. That two-faced Ashraf need not think he could say bad things about people's dads in the playground, and be friends with them straight away in the class. He needn't think that, because it wasn't going to happen.

A sudden thought struck him. Actually though, actually, I'm not going to care any more what that lot say! I'm going to be friends with them, but I'm not going to care any more what they say – why should I? I got something to look forward to now, that nobody else knows about. And they're not going to know about it, neither, because they don't deserve to!

. . . It's not right what I thought before, it's not really Kate Jackson's fault that I can't tell about

187

her brother-in-law. And I'm sorry for her, really, because that Frank is guilty, and my dad is innocent. And they can't prove he isn't, because he *is*. *My dad is innocent.* Suddenly the thought gave Desmond tremendous pride, and he grinned, baring the broken tooth. 'What are you writing about then, Des?' said Ashraf, mistaking the grin.

'Belt up!' said Desmond, with savage hostility.

In her seat, Kate stared at a blank page with unseeing eyes. It's terrible what's happening at home, she thought, *terrible*. It looks like Dawn isn't never going to stop crying. And my dad won't say nothing excepting *we're going to get throwed out*. And as for my mum, I don't think I like her any more at all, she is too cruel to Dawn. Fancy shouting at her and telling her not to cry because Frank isn't worth it! I know he isn't worth it, but Dawn can still cry, can't she?

And Dawn won't talk to me because I told, and I don't blame her. Perhaps I didn't ought to have told, I don't know. Perhaps it was all my fault . . . I don't want it to be my fault! It is terrible for Dawn now, because the baby is coming soon, and Frank won't be there. The baby won't have a dad now. I can't bear to think about Dawn's baby that won't have a dad. . . . And Frank won't see the baby when it's born, but I'm not sorry for Frank, because he told a lot of lies. I don't like lies. And he broke his promise as well. He made a promise to me and he broke it!

I am sorry for Dawn, though, and nobody is being nice to Dawn, and I wish she would talk to me so I could be nice to her, but she won't. I would tell her I'm sorry, only I think she won't listen.

I could write a letter to her. I know, I could make

her a *card*! . . . Mrs Warren isn't looking, I could do it now! Mrs Warren is so busy looking at everybody's work, she has forgot about me, I think. Hooray, I can make the card for Dawn now!

Brilliant!

Kate sidled out of her seat, and fetched her felt-tipped pens from her tray. She took a blank sheet of paper from Mrs Warren's table, as well. She folded the paper, and chewed her hair, and wriggled the glasses up and down on her nose. Then she made a barricade of books, so Suzette and Nasreen and Faridah wouldn't be able to see what she was doing.

On the front of the card, Kate drew a large lopsided heart. She coloured the heart carefully in red, then pierced it with an arrow. At one end of the arrow she wrote DAWN, and at the other end KATE. Then she decorated the whole page with flowers – blue, pink and orange.

The effect was pretty. Kate opened the card, and chewed her hair thoughtfully, while she decided what to put inside. At last, using a different colour for each letter, Kate wrote *Dear Dawn I am sorry about what happened. and I am sad about what happened. and I love you. From Kate xxxxxxxxxxxxxxx.*

'Are you doing some work at last, Kate?' came Mrs Warren's voice from across the room.

She was coming, she was coming! Mrs Warren was coming, and she was going to see! Alarmed, Kate stuffed the card under her jumper.

'What are you hiding? Give that to me!'

Kate clutched herself around the middle, to protect the card under her jumper. Mrs Warren was going to see the card, and she mustn't, because it was private! Mrs Warren mustn't see the card she

189

made for Dawn, and the class mustn't see it neither, because if they did they would guess her secret, perhaps! Kate doubled over, and wrapped her arms tighter, around her stomach.

'Whatever is the matter with you today?' said Mrs Warren.

'I think she got a belly-ache,' said Suzette.

'I have, I have, I got all bad pains. Oo-oo-ooh!'

'Oh dear, you *are* in a bad way,' Mrs Warren teased her. Mrs Warren did not believe in Kate's pains for one minute, but she was very much aware that *something* was wrong. She must be gentle, and she must be tactful, to make up for all those times in the past weeks when she had been neither. And she would keep an eye on Kate. If Kate's behaviour didn't improve, Mrs Warren would make a real effort to get to the bottom of it. Tactfully, of course.

'Oh-oo-ooh! I want to go to the toilet!'

'Go on then,' said Mrs Warren. 'Perhaps you'll manage to be more yourself when you come back.'

'She's doing it for attention,' said Natasha.

Kate sped to the cloakroom, and hid the precious card in her coat pocket. She had to fold it up rather small to do that, so it would be creased, but never mind. It would be all right with Dawn now, the card would put it right, so there would be one good thing at least.

'Right!' said Mrs Warren, as Kate returned to the classroom. 'Is this, by any chance, the Kate Jackson we all know and love?'

'I think so,' said Kate, with a little watery smile.

Desmond frowned in his seat, and prodded the broken tooth with his finger.

At dinner time, and after school, the gossiping

and sniggering went on. Even Kate, isolated in her anguish as she was, could not fail to know what the nasty little groups were saying.

That's why Frank was so scared yesterday, she thought! Because he knows the police got their eye on him. But all the class are saying it's Desmond's dad again. It's terrible, and I hate them, and they would talk about me like that if they knew! . . . It's terrible for Desmond, I feel awful, and I ought to feel more awful about Desmond but I can't, it's too much for me. I haven't got any room for thinking about Desmond today, I only have room for thinking about poor, poor Dawn!

She hurried home, her heart thumping, through the cold streets.

Dawn and Dad were sitting in separate seats, not looking at one another. Dad's bronchitis had got worse again. He coughed and retched and looked sorry for himself. Dawn just looked desperately lonely. She still sobbed, in a hopeless sort of way, but otherwise the room was unnaturally quiet; the television was getting a well-earned rest.

Suddenly shy, Kate stood by the door, awkwardly fingering the folded paper in her pocket. She stood on one leg, and then on the other.

Dawn looked at Kate, fidgeting by the door. 'You satisfied now, then?' she said, bitterly. She had taken the bracelet off, at last.

'Satisfied about what?'

'Satisfied with all the damage you done.'

Kate pulled out the card, grubby now as well as creased, and dropped it into Dawn's lap.

'What's this?'

'It's for you.'

Dawn opened it listlessly, read it without

expression, then brushed it with the back of her hand on to the seat beside her.

'Don't you like it?'

'It's all right,' said Dawn, in a sullen voice.

But presently her hand strayed back to the paper, and she read it again, the tears seeping down her cheeks.

'If I could make it all not happen I would,' said Kate, earnestly. 'If I could have a punishment that would make it not happen I wouldn't mind.'

'Why should you be punished?' said Dawn, without interest.

'It was my fault.'

'No, it wasn't.'

'Wasn't it?'

'No. I just said that. I know you couldn't help what Frank done. I know that really.'

'*Thank* you!' Kate's face beamed her gratitude.

'We're going to get throwed out now anyway,' said Dad. 'Whoever's fault it was.'

'Is that all you can think about?' said Kate.

'What's the matter with this house today?' said Mum. 'What's the matter, then, somebody died?'

'In a way,' said Dawn.

'Don't tell me you're still mooning over that little tea-leaf!'

'I think she still loves him,' said Kate.

'Who asked you?' said Mum. 'What's wrong with the telly, then? Telly on the blink?'

Dad shrugged, and no one else answered.

'Everybody got the laryngitis as well, I see,' said Mum. 'Everybody got paralysis of the vocal chords. As well as everybody forgot how to smile.'

'You can't expect us to be *happy*!' said Kate.

'Well, *I'm* happy,' Mum declared. 'I'm happy we found out that little weasel in time. Scheming little toad! You lot want to count your blessings, you don't know when you had a lucky escape.'

'We're still going to get throwed out, though,' said Dad. 'Most likely. When the police come.'

'Oh, shut your cake-hole!' said Mum.

Mum turned on the television and began shrieking with laughter at a not-very-funny situation comedy.

'I think I'll go to bed,' said Dawn.

'That's right, you go,' said Mum. 'One long face out the way, anyhow!'

'Kate . . .' said Dawn.

'What?'

'How about you come and sleep with me tonight?' She was half embarrassed to be asking it, but desperate not to be alone.

'Do you really want me to?' said Kate, flushing with pleasure.

'Yeah, I do.'

'Good idea,' said Mum. 'We can make that a permanent arrangement from now.'

Dawn and Kate cuddled warmly in the double bed. 'Did Frank tell you where he was going, in the end?' said Kate.

'Yes, but I'm not supposed to say.'

'Is it a secret?'

'. . . I'm not supposed to tell anybody.'

'I bet he's gone to that Spotted Dick,' said Kate, bitterly.

'No he hasn't then. He's gone to South America.'

'Oh yeah – they always go there, don't they? Robbers, I mean. They always go to South

America; I seen it on the telly. Anyway, now you give away the secret.'

'Actually,' said Dawn. 'I think it wasn't a true secret. I think Frank told a lie.'

'*Didn't* he go to South America, then?'

'I can't see it, can you? He never been abroad anywhere, not even to France. Anyway, he hasn't got a passport.'

'Couldn't he get one?'

'I don't think so,' said Dawn. She pondered for a bit, twisting her wedding ring round and round her finger. '. . . Actually, I think I can guess where he *did* go,' she said.

'To his mum's?'

'Nah – I think the police could easy find him at his mum's. I think he most likely went to his dad.'

'I forgot he had a dad,' said Kate.

'That's 'cos he hardly ever goes there.'

'Do you think he would tell his dad what he done?' Kate wondered.

'I think he would have to. I can't think of any excuse he could make, can you?'

'Not really.'

'The only thing is, I don't know about his step-mum. I don't know if she would let him hide in the house.'

'*I* think she would let him hide,' said Kate. 'Everybody is not as hard hearted as our mum, you know.'

'There is *her* mum as well, though, that lives with them.'

'But it's all part of the same family, isn't it?' Kate reasoned. 'They would stand up for Frank because he is their family. They would hide him, and not let the police find him, because he is their family, and you have to do that.'

'Yeah – that's right!' said Dawn. 'Yeah, you're right, Kate, I'm sure you're right. . . . Do you know what I just thought of? I think them at his dad's wouldn't blame Frank like our mum did. I think they would say it was mostly Spotted Dick's fault.'

'It *was* really, wasn't it, Dawn? It *was* Spotted Dick's fault.'

'I *hate* Spotted Dick!'

'So do I,' said Kate.

'Wait for me!'

Kate heard Desmond's footsteps pounding close behind her, and she began to run. It was many days since they had walked together, going to school or going home. Kate certainly didn't want to start that again *now*.

'No, wait, wait!' He caught her up. 'I want to talk to you.' He sounded quite excited.

'What about?'

'About old Ma Harris's burglary.'

As though it could be about anything else! Why must Desmond talk to her about it, though? Suddenly a terrible thought struck Kate; a possibility she had quite overlooked in the anguish of yesterday. 'Did you tell, then?' She didn't dare look at his face.

'Did I tell what?'

'About Frank, did you tell?'

'*No!*'

Kate burst into tears.

'I *told* you I wouldn't tell! What you keep on saying I'm going to tell, for?' He was all the more indignant because he had indeed considered doing just that, fleetingly, yesterday.

'Don't you want to clear your dad, then?'

'My dad *is* clear. Anyway, they can't say he done *this* one!'

'How can your dad be clear, though, if you didn't tell on Frank?'

'Ah-ha! You don't know, do you?'

'Know what?'

'Who it was done the burglary in Mrs Harris's house!'

Kate swallowed, and pushed the glasses up to wipe her eyes. 'Of course I know. And I trusted him, and I didn't ought to have done it, like you said. He broke his promise, and he went and killed poor Bruce.'

'Oh, Bruce ain't *dead*.'

'Isn't he? Jacob said he was. He said it, he said it!'

'Jacob got it wrong, then, because they only knocked him out.'

'*Oh*.'

'And *you* got it wrong, because you thought it was Frank done it, didn't you? And it wasn't! . . . And I got it wrong as well,' he admitted. 'But I know the truth of it now.'

Kate gaped at him. Her head was spinning, she thought it very likely she was going to faint.

'The police got both of them, you know.'

'Both of who?'

'Guess!'

'I don't want to guess, I want you to tell me! Desmond, please tell me who the police have got both of. Tell me quickly, *please*.'

'All right, I will. I will, and you are going to be

196

very happy about this, Kate. It was . . . wait for it . . . it was . . . SCRUFFY and BAD NEWS!'

'*What*?' Kate whispered. 'Are you *sure*?'

'I'm sure, I'm sure, I couldn't be more sure! My dad told me, he heard about it in the pub. They got Bad News first, and he grassed on Scruffy, and they got Scruffy yesterday evening. It was a lot of fun when the police come to get him. He was shouting and yelling he was going to kill Bad News for grassing, and all of Somerset Gardens come out to watch.'

She had forgotten all about those two! Since she found out about Frank, Kate had not given Scruffy and Bad News another thought. Without a word, now, Kate began to run – blindly, bumping into things – away from Desmond, away from the truth, away from herself.

In school, she acted almost normally. She made herself do it, she had to – because people would catch on something was wrong if she didn't. So Kate worked, and went swimming with her class, and skipped with Suzette in the playground, and even Mrs Warren was fooled. Dear Mrs Warren, her old caring self again at last!

To begin with, it seemed to Kate as though someone else was doing the working, and skipping, and so on. As though someone else had been wound up like clockwork, to do those things instead of her. But as the day wore on, it was the Kate in school who was really her; and the other Kate, the one who had terrible things to face, was somebody she needn't be, and didn't have to think about, until it was time to go home.

197

At home time, Desmond grabbed the back of Kate's coat.

'Let me go! I got to get home!'

'What's the matter with you?'

'Nothing!' Frantically, Kate tried to pull away from him.

'You should be happy, why aren't you happy, then?' He himself was extremely happy, now everyone knew who had been doing all these burglaries. . . . Well, anyway, they *thought* they knew, which was good enough for that lot! The main thing was, nobody was saying bad things about his dad any more. 'Why ain't you happy, Kate?' he said, again.

'I *am* happy.'

'I don't think you are, then. Your face doesn't look right.'

'It's none of your business what my face looks like.'

'All right, *be* like that!'

'Something dreadful!' said Kate, in the house.

'What now?' There was terror on Dawn's face. She didn't think she could bear any more.

'Is it the police?' said Dad, fearfully.

'No. That's not the dreadful thing. The dreadful thing is, I made a mistake.'

'What mistake?'

'It wasn't Frank done Mrs Harris's burglary, it was somebody else. Frank kept his promise all the time, and I thought he never!'

'How do you know it was somebody else?'

'They got arrested. Desmond told me. And Bruce isn't dead after all.'

'Are you sure?' It was too good to be true. They

were not about to be evicted after all. Dad was afraid to let himself believe it.

'Yes, I'm sure, I'm sure. He isn't dead, he was only knocked out.'

'I don't mean *that*,' said Dad.

'But you told for nothing!' said Dawn.

'I know.' Kate was so wretched she wanted to die. 'I'm a bad person! I'm bad! I should have thought, and I didn't! I just didn't think of it, that it could be somebody else.'

'You jump to conclusions! You jump to conclusions too much!'

'I know.' It was like the telly man, all over again, only this time worse. A million times worse.

'You told on Frank for nothing! Our mum throw him out for nothing!'

'I know. I'm sorry, I'm sorry.'

'I hate you!'

'I know you hate me,' said Kate. 'I hate myself. I told on Frank, and I didn't ought to have done it, because he kept his promise all the time!'

'It's all your fault Frank went away! It's all your fault!'

'I know.'

'It's all your fault! I hate you! It's all your fault!'

'I know. . . . And he went away and he thinks I thought that terrible thing about him.'

'Oh, *that*!' said Dawn, impatiently.

'I hurt him, though. I hurt him in his feelings.'

'Never mind his feelings! What about me? I lost my husband, you know. Near enough.'

'But Mum will have to let him come back, now. When we tell her about the mistake.'

'She won't.'

'She will! She will have to!'

Dawn's tears subsided, just a little bit. 'Even if she does, I shall never forgive *you*!'

'What you take me for?' said Mum. 'A idiot?'

'Told you!' said Dawn, bitterly.

'But he never done it!' Kate persisted. 'You don't understand, I made a mistake.'

'What about all the other times?'

'That's right,' said Dad, in fresh alarm. 'The police can still come because of the other times.'

'Anyway, I'm not having that tea-leaf in my house again, I don't trust him.'

'He won't do it no more,' said Dawn.

'He won't' said Kate. 'He promised, you know. *Please*, Mum. *Please!*'

'A leopard don't change its spots.'

Dawn began to cry noisily. 'And shut up that noise!' Mum told her. 'I'm sick of your whingeing.'

'But I *love* him!'

'Love? You don't know the meaning of the word! You love yourself, that's who you love!'

'You see, Dawnie,' Dad explained. 'If we have Frank back, he can still get us throwed out.'

'Are you coming to bed, Kate?' said Dawn, in a small voice.

'Do you still want me, then?'

'I haven't got anybody else on my side, have I?'

13

The adventure that went all wrong

'I should have went with him!' Dawn lamented. 'I should have went with him. It was our mum's fault. She made me not go with Frank. It wasn't my fault; it was hers!'

'What about the baby, though?' said Kate, doubtfully. 'The baby is going to be born soon.'

'Oh, yeah. Well, afterwards. Afterwards I could go to Frank, couldn't I?'

'You don't know where he is, though.'

'I think I do, you know. And I *do* want to see him. I miss him. I want to give him a hug, and tell him I still love him.'

'I wish I could see him too,' said Kate. 'I wish I could tell him I made a mistake. I wish I could put it right. I keep seeing his face, when I said that terrible thing. I can't stop seeing his face.'

'. . . Kate, I had a idea.'

'What's that?'

'You know I said I think I know where Frank could be?'

'At his dad's?'

'I'm sure that's it, I'm really sure.'

'He might be just sleeping on the streets. In a cardboard box.'

'Not *Frank*.'

'Where does his dad live, then?'

'He lives at Bow. It's a long way. Right the other side of London. In the East End. I can't remember

the name of the road, I think it was *Ben* something.
I only went there once. A long time ago, before we
was married, even.'

'So will you go now? And look for it? Is that your
idea?'

'*Kate*! . . . I can't! . . . Not with this lump!'

'So?'

'Well – what's wrong with *you* going?'

'*Me*?'

'Yeah – go and find Frank, and give him a hug
from me!' She would hardly have said *that*, a few
days ago!

'By myself, though? Go by myself?'

'Well *I* can't go, can I?' said Dawn, piteously.
'You can't expect *me* to go!'

'But you can't expect me to neither!' said Kate
in panic. 'Not all by myself!'

'Don't you want to put it right, then?' Dawn's
voice had risen to a whine. 'You said you wanted
to put it right. You did say that, Kate.'

'I *can't* put it right, though. How can I put it
right? Anyway, he might not want to see me!'

'He will, he will!'

'He might be angry with me, for telling on him.'

'He won't, he won't! And you will have the
chance to tell him you're sorry what you thought,'
Dawn wheedled. 'And you can tell him I haven't
forgot him. And you can tell him the police caught
the ones that did Mrs Harris's house, so they ain't
going to blame him for it.'

'What about the other things he done?'

'I know. That is the problem.'

Kate considered. 'Don't you think God will have
forgive him, though?'

'What you mean?'

202

'I mean, I was thinking before, if Frank would go straight, God would not let the police come after him.'

'Yeah, yeah. I could write him a letter, couldn't I? And you could take it. I could make him a card, like you done for me, and put the letter inside.'

Kate said nothing.

'I could, couldn't I, Kate?'

Kate turned over, and lay with her back to Dawn, her mind racing.

In the morning, Dawn started again. 'I been thinking about that letter, I'm going to write to Frank.'

'I can't go, Dawn, I can't! Not all by myself! Anyway, our mum would kill me.'

'She wouldn't have to know. You could bunk off school, how about that?'

'You told of me when I done that before.'

'Well, I won't this time, will I? You can get there and back before she comes home, easy. You can get back by four o'clock, in fact, so it looks like you just come home from school. *Two* o'clock more like it, so you will have to hang about a bit.'

'How will I know where to go?'

'It's Benfield Road. I think that's right. I remembered it in the night.'

'But how will I get there?'

'You go to Bow Station. On the Underground train. I'll give you the money for the ticket.'

'But I never went on the Underground by myself before.'

'Well, you have to learn how to do it some time.'

'Will I have to change trains? I don't know how to change trains. I shall get all muddled up, in the passages.'

'No, you won't.'

'Anyway, what will I do when I get to the station?'

'Easy. Ask somebody where Benfield Road is.'

'Suppose it's not Benfield Road? Suppose it's something else?'

'I'm sure it's Benfield Road . . . or it might be Benfield Street. Go on, Kate! I have to have *somebody* to take my letter!'

'Why couldn't you put the letter in the post box?'

'Because I don't know the proper address.'

'Well, *I* don't know the proper address. It might be Benfield Road or it might be another name. And anyway I don't know the number of the house.'

'You could find it if you go there, though. It's got a green door. Anyway, it's not far from the station.'

Desmond had been thinking quite a lot about Kate. There was something funny that he didn't understand. She should have been overjoyed at his news yesterday, and she wasn't! There was some terrible trouble he didn't know about, there must be. And he didn't like the thought of Kate having some terrible trouble. She didn't deserve it! All that time she was standing in his way he kept forgetting what a nice person she was, but he remembered it now.

Anyway, she was worth a lot more than those boys – Curtis, and that lot – those so-called friends that turned against him, and made fun of him, every time there was something new to whisper about! Kate was worth more than that, and she deserved to have good things happen to her, not bad. . . . If only he could find out what the trouble was.

Desmond dawdled in Wessex Road, waiting to catch Kate on the way to school.

'Hi.'

'Hi.' Her voice was stiff, without warmth. Desmond trailed along, just behind her.

'You don't want to talk to me, do you?'

'Not much.'

Desmond veered away from her into the road. He made a large half circle, to meet up with Kate again on the pavement. 'Remember when we done that detecting?'

'Yes.'

'It was fun, wasn't it? Remember when we went on the swings?'

'Yes.'

'That was fun as well. Shall we go and have some more fun one day, like that?' He said the words looking straight ahead, only glancing round for a moment afterwards.

'I don't feel like having fun.' The sad little sentence spilled out, into the bleak and sunless morning.

'So what *do* you feel like doing?'

'. . . I can't tell you.'

'I thought you were going to say that. I think it's something to do with that Frank.'

'. . . I can't talk about it. It's too complicated.'

'O.K., it's up to you.'

At home time he dawdled again, just in front of her. He dawdled and dawdled, until she just *had* to catch up. They walked, stealing wary glances at one another.

'. . . Desmond,' said Kate.

'What?'

'Are you my friend, then?'

'Yep.'

'Do you mean it? Are you *really* my friend?'

'. . . Yep.'

'. . . It isn't going to be exactly *fun*.'

Desmond poked at the broken tooth. 'What isn't?'

'Actually, it's hard. I don't think you will want to.'

'I'm not afraid of hard things.'

'I know. But it's a long way.'

'What is?'

'Bow. I have to go to Bow, and I'm scared to go by myself.'

'Why, where is it, then? This Bow?'

'It's all the way to the East End,' said Kate, 'I have to go and look for Frank.'

'I thought it was *something* to do with him,' said Desmond, pleased at being right. 'I thought that yesterday. I guessed it!'

'I have to bunk off school tomorrow. I have to take a letter from Dawn. And I have to tell Frank I made a mistake. I thought he killed Mrs Harris's dog, only he never, and I have to tell him.'

Desmond was silent, poking at the broken tooth. 'I best come with you, then,' he said, at last.

'You don't have to.'

'I know I don't have to.'

'You could get in trouble, you know.'

'Shut up! I can get in trouble if I want to!' The urge to look after her had never been stronger; to look after her, and keep the bad things away from her, because she couldn't do it for herself. 'You can't go by yourself, can you? It's not safe; you trust people too much. You will talk to Strangers or something.'

206

'It's not the Strangers, it's the passages. I don't like the passages in the Underground. I don't know which ones to go in.'

'That's all right. Leave it to me.' Poor, soft Kate, scared of the passages! *He* wasn't scared of the passages! The passages would be easy peasy, he was sure.

'Do you know how to do it, then?'

'Of course!'

'You went on the Underground before? By yourself?'

'A load of times!'

To be strictly accurate, he had done it twice. Two stops down the line. With no changes at all.

'You won the Pools or something, Kate?' said Mum, suspiciously.

'No. I'm just feeling a little bit happy.'

'Well, that makes a change. The rest of you still afraid of cracking your faces, I see! . . . What's Lady Muck looking so sly about?'

'Nothing,' said Dawn. 'I'm not.'

'Oh? Must be something wrong with my eyesight, then. I best go down the opticians. Get some glasses. I think I'll have them butterfly ones. With the glitter bits . . . . Somethink funny?'

'Do you have to smile so much?' said Dawn, in the bedroom. 'I think you're going to give it away.'

'I can't help it,' said Kate, beaming. 'I'm going to see Frank, tomorrow. And I'm not scared a bit, now. Now Desmond is coming with me, I'm not scared; I'm looking forward to it. The only thing is, I don't know how I'm going to find the house.'

'Oh, that's *easy*,' said Dawn. She was happy too,

now; her faith and her hopes were all pinned on her letter. 'You don't have to make a fuss about a easy thing like that. The thing is, there isn't hardly any houses at Bow.'

'Not any *houses*?'

'It's all flats. Everywhere you go it's flats. But Frank's dad got a little house all in between the flats. There's not many houses in the row, so you can easy find which one is his. It's got a green door, remember!'

Kate was reassured to learn how easy it was going to be to find Frank's dad's house. The last of her worries swept away, Kate turned over in bed, and prepared for sleep.

'Now I better tell you how to go on the Underground,' said Dawn.

'It's all right, Desmond knows about that.'

'I have to tell you which station, though. It's Bow. No, it's Bow Road, I think. Anyway, you can see it on the map.'

'Desmond will understand the map. He's done it loads of times.'

'You might as well listen to me as well,' Dawn persisted. 'All the lines have different colours. I forget which colour is which.'

'Desmond will know,' said Kate, sleepily.

'Bow is on the District Line, I think. Our one is the Bakerloo, so you have to change.'

'It's all right. Desmond will know how to do it. He's done it *loads* of times.'

Kate came out into freezing fog, and met Desmond outside the station. It was good about the fog, he said. The fog would stop people from seeing them not going to school.

208

The children stood by the map on the station platform; it looked very complicated. 'The different colours are for the different lines,' said Kate.

'I know!' said Desmond. 'I know!'

'Our one is the Bakerloo.'

'I know it is.'

'Which colour is it for the Bakerloo?'

'Belt up, Frog! Give me a chance. I'm just trying to work it out.'

Kate peered through the crooked glasses. 'There's our station, look! I found it!'

'*I* found it ages ago.'

'So the Bakerloo is brown.'

'I was just going to say that.'

'Can you find Bow Road?'

'Not yet,' Desmond admitted. 'There's so many.'

'It's on the District Line,' said Kate. 'Oh, look, Desmond! There's a thing at the bottom that tells you which colour is for which line. The District Line is green!'

'Of course it is,' said Desmond. 'It's always green for the District Line.'

'So now we have to look for where they meet. The green one and the brown one. Is that how you do it, Desmond?'

'Yep. That's how you do it.'

But Desmond's confidence was fading fast. So many lines, so many colours. Threatened with failure, he struggled to make sense of the map, his thinking confused now.

'Looks like we have to change at Paddington,' said Kate.

'Yeah,' said Desmond, sourly.

Getting to Paddington was no problem, but the next two or three hours were a nightmare. First they got muddled up in the passages. Next they went all the way to Wimbledon, miles and miles in the wrong direction. And then they found themselves on a train that went round and round in a circle, and brought them back to Paddington again.

Each time they made a mistake, Desmond's temper grew worse, and finally he mutinied. They would have to give up, he said, and go home. It was no use Kate blaming him though, because it wasn't his fault; it was the Underground people's fault for making it so hard.

Kate was frantic. 'But we can't give up; we can't. Let's ask someone.'

'You're not allowed to talk to Strangers.'

'Oh, yeah. There must be some way, though. What about that train man over there, let's ask him! A train man is not a Stranger.'

The train man put them right.

Through the tunnels again, a long long way, and at last they were climbing the steps at Bow Road station. 'What a dump!' said Desmond, not disposed to be much pleased with anything he saw, after losing so much face this morning, and not being the one to think of asking the train man.

'I don't mind if it's a dump,' said Kate. 'It's where Frank is! . . . Tra-la-la!' she sang. 'We got to Frank's station at last.'

The cold struck at them as they came into the street. Fog hung whitely over tall buildings, and the streaking traffic on a wide, heartless road. Kate felt very small, suddenly, and lost. She squinted sideways at Desmond, who was poking at the broken tooth with his finger. 'Right!' he said, still sulking. 'Where is this place we have to go?'

'I don't know. I know it's not far from the station.'

'So what is the address?'

'I don't know.'

'You don't know the *address*?'

'Dawn said it's Benfield Road. . . . It's all right, we can ask someone. Someone will know.'

'They're all Strangers, though. You can't ask Strangers.'

That again! 'How we ever going to find it, then, if we aren't allowed to ask?' The cold was eating through Kate's coat, gnawing at her legs, burrowing into her shoes. And Desmond had come all this way with her, but she almost wished he hadn't, because he wasn't being helpful at all, he was just being obstructive and difficult.

A police car drew up, and stopped further down the road. 'I know!' said Kate. 'I know, Desmond, we could ask the police.'

'NO!'

'Why not? I think that was a good idea I had. The police aren't Strangers, are they?'

'Don't be stupid! They will ask us why we aren't in school. Remember the park?'

'Oh, right!' How could she have forgotten? How could she have forgotten the sad fact that the police were not her friends any more? The sorrow was a new weight on her spirits; Kate sighed.

'Come on, then!' said Desmond, roughly.

'Come on where?'

'What you think? Look for Benfield Road, innit!'

They trailed the streets for an hour. They found a police station, which made Kate nervous, and a cemetery beyond that, but no Benfield Road. They found Ben*worth* Road, but there were no little houses in it, only flats. Desmond began to complain that he was hungry – at which point Kate realized that it was past dinner time, and the afternoon already! Panic crept upwards – through her knees, and her stomach, and into her chest. She took the sandwiches and the orange juice out of her school bag, and thrust them at Desmond.

'Don't *you* want any?'

'I couldn't swallow nothing, I don't think.'

Desmond looked at her. He saw how pinched and desperate her face had become, and he began to be ashamed of his surliness. Awkwardly, he put a hand on Kate's shoulder. 'Don't worry. We'll look for some more in a minute.'

They trudged again, with tired and aching legs, and everywhere they went the tall flats loomed at them, menacingly, out of the fog. They ventured further – a good way from the station this time, in case Dawn forgot how far it was really, but there was no Benfield Road anywhere. 'We shall have to give up,' said Desmond, at last. 'Your stupid sister must have got it wrong.'

'No!'

'It's getting late.'

'It's not, it's not!'

'Come on, Kate, let's go home.'

'NO!'

'All right, all right. We'll look a little bit longer.'

They did, but hope was seeping away. All Kate's hopes – first a trickle, then a stream, then a flood, pouring into the foggy street, leaving her drained and empty. 'If only you would let us ask someone,' she said in a small flat voice.

'Do you want us to be kidnapped then? Is that what you want?'

'No.' He was probably right. In any case, she was too tired to fight his will.

'Come on. We're going home. We have to.'

'All right.'

She trailed behind him, feeling quite dead inside. And at the station she came suddenly, shakily, alive again. 'Desmond, look!'

'What at?'

'That paper man! A paper man is not a Stranger! Oh, let's ask the paper man Desmond, *please*.'

He hesitated, torn between a fixed idea and the needs of this very special situation.

'*Please*, Desmond!'

'. . . All right, all right. *I'll* do it. Just this once, mind!'

'No Benfield Road round here,' said the paper man.

'See?' said Desmond. 'Your stupid sister got it wrong, like I said.'

'Ben *some*thing then,' said Kate, desperately. 'Oh please, please think!'

The paper man scratched his head. 'Are you sure you don't mean *Den*field?'

'No,' said Kate 'It's got to begin with *Ben*.'

'You can't be sure of that,' said Desmond. 'You can't be sure of *nothing* your stupid sister said!'

'Oh.' Kate's head was spinning as she tried to readjust her thoughts. 'Is it far?' she said with a thumping heart to the paper man.

'Nah! About five minutes,' he told them. 'Straight down there, second left.'

'Oh, come on, come on, Desmond!' Kate began to run.

Desmond started to run after her, then turned

213

back. 'What time is it, actually?' he asked the paper man.

The paper man looked at his watch. 'Just coming up for four.'

Desmond pounded after Kate, and caught her by the arm. 'Kate, we have to go home!'

'*No!*'

'We have to, Kate! You know how long it took to get here. If we don't go soon, we won't even be home before your mum, I don't think!'

'But we can't give up now!'

'What about if we come back another day?'

'No, now, now!'

Desmond shrugged. 'All right. It's you that's going to get the hit off of your mum!' He would get one from his own mum, most likely, but the main thing was, he couldn't be cruel. Kate was bursting, just about, with eagerness and hope; it would be cruel to stop her now.

They hurried through the fog, and found Denfield Road, just as the paper man had said. They had passed the little turning before, in their search, but the end of the sign was broken, and since the name didn't begin with a B, they hadn't bothered trying to read it. There was a row of little houses, though and, oh joy, joy, one of them had a green door!

Kate ran up and knocked. There was a bell beside the door, so she rang that as well. Then she knocked again. 'All right, all right, coming!' came Frank's voice, from inside.

The door opened. Frank's mouth dropped open as well. 'It's *me*!' said Kate, with a tremulous smile, and eyes full of love.

Frank did not smile back.

'It's me,' said Kate again.

'What you doing here?' He spoke roughly, without welcome; he was clearly dismayed to see her.

Kate faltered. 'I – I come to tell you I made a mistake.'

'Yes, you did. You made a mistake coming here. Go home!'

He was angry with her after all! He was angry because she told! She looked up at him sorrowfully, pleading his forgiveness. 'Please let me put it right! I can't put it right if you won't listen to me.'

'There's nothing to put right! It's nothing to do with you! Go home and keep out of it!' He ran a hand through his curls, making them stand on end. His face was flushed, his eyes bright and hot. He looked like a naughty child, caught out and frightened.

'I don't understand—'

'You don't have to understand! It's nothing to do with you, it's between me and Dawn, so just go!'

'Who is it at the door?' said a voice from inside.

'Nobody!' said Frank to the voice. His words came out in a high-pitched croak; he sounded almost hysterical. 'Go *home*!' he hissed again, at Kate.

Kate took the letter from Dawn out of her school bag. She held it out to Frank, but he made no move to take it.

'It's from Dawn.'

'Put it away, I don't want it!'

'But it's to tell you she loves you!'

'Well I don't love her!' Frank squeaked. 'I finished with her. I don't want to see her, and I don't want to see you, and I told you that before. So go! Go on, go home, and don't come back!'

215

There was a frantic note in his voice now, as he slammed the door right in Kate's face.

Kate stood for a moment, frozen to the step with shock. Then she turned a stricken face to Desmond, still waiting by the gate. And Desmond had no words. He was too upset and hurt for Kate to have words, but he put his hand on her shoulder again and steered her towards the station.

Kate stumbled mutely along, her shoulder under Desmond's hand. 'If the trains are quick we could still get home in time.' His voice came thickly, with effort.

Kate said nothing.

'We could get home before your mum, perhaps. So you won't get in trouble.'

Kate said nothing.

'Get home before your mum, eh? Shall we try and do that?'

They were outside the station, now. The paper man waved at them, not noticing anything was wrong – and went back to serving some customers. 'I can't go home!' said Kate, suddenly.

'Yes you can. Of course you can!'

Desmond tried to push her through the entrance, but she grabbed at the wall and refused to budge. 'I can't! I can't go home and tell Dawn that, no way!' The pathetic letter was still in her hand.

'Say we never found the house.'

'I can't! I can't hide that, it's too much for me!'

'Let's talk about it on the train.'

No answer.

'Kate? Come on, let's talk about it on the train!'

No answer.

'*Kate*!'

She ducked then, suddenly, escaping from his

216

hand. Dismayed, Desmond watched her run, down the road and into the fog. It was several moments before he had recovered from his surprise enough to follow her.

He was just in time to see her turn, plunging down the road that led to the police station, and the cemetery. What did she think she was doing? Where did she think she was going? Desmond pounded after her, and caught her up near the bottom. He grabbed her coat.

'Leave me!' She wrenched away from him, and he was astonished at the strength in her writhing arms. 'Leave me!' Something wild in her voice alarmed him; he was afraid to grab at her again. He stood hesitating, not knowing what to do, as she ran from him once more, through the fog, now rapidly swallowing up the light, and right through the gate in the railings that led into the cemetery.

There was no one but Desmond to see her go. No one but Desmond to follow her, stumbling and hurrying, deeper and deeper, very much afraid of losing track of her, among the bushes and the tombstones. 'Kate! Where are you?'

Silence. He had lost her, he *had*. In a nightmare he plunged round and around, calling and listening. Everywhere was the raw, still smell of cold earth, but no sound.

'*Kate*!' There was a rustle, faint and stealthy, a little way to his right. Desmond trod through dead twigs and found her at last, crouched behind someone's grave, her knees hugged to her chest, rocking.

'What are you doing?'

No answer.

'*Kate*! What you think you're *doing*?'

No answer.

Desmond crouched beside her, and put a hand tentatively on her shoulder. With a violent movement, she wrenched away again.

'Kate! Come on!'

She would not look at him, she would not speak to him. Desmond moved away and sat on the next-door gravestone, prodding at his broken tooth. It was bitterly cold. The fog wrapped him in loneliness, freezing his thoughts. He sat, and prodded the tooth, and sat some more.

'Kate!' he tried for the twentieth time. 'Are you sick?'

No answer.

'Are you sick, or something?'

Still no answer. Stiff with cold, in spite of his quilted anorak, Desmond heaved himself off his gravestone and moved towards her once more. 'Kate!' He looked down at the huddled figure, but she gave no sign that she was aware of him standing there. Her coat was smart, but not very warm, and she had had nothing to eat all day. In what was left of the light, her hands looked blue.

Desmond bent suddenly, and grabbed her by the armpits. 'Come on!' he shouted. 'Come on, we're going home!'

He yanked her to her feet and began to pull her by one arm, forcing her to take a few stumbling steps after him. She tried to unclasp his hands, but his grip was too strong. She fought him silently as he pulled her, over the rough ground, back to the nearest path.

The going would have been easier then, only Kate suddenly went limp, sagging towards the ground, so Desmond had to get her by the armpits again and drag the dead weight of her, backwards,

218

right up to the railings at last. He held her against the gate with his body, while he struggled with one hand to open the gate.

The gate would not move.

The gate would not move, because it was locked!

14

Missing

'Where's Kate?' said Dad, suddenly. 'She ain't come in from school yet, has she?'

Dawn shrugged, uneasily. 'Probably mucking about the streets with that Desmond.'

'In this fog, though?'

'She'll show up in a minute.'

'She didn't ought to worry us like this.'

The doorbell rang. 'There she is,' said Dawn, hiding her relief.

'And about time,' said Dad.

'Lost her key, I suppose.'

'She's a naughty girl!'

'You going to let her in, then?' said Dawn.

'It's cold out there,' Dad complained.

'It's cold for everybody, not just you.'

'Go on, Dawnie.'

The bell rang again. Dad hugged his blanket more firmly round him. With a bad grace, Dawn heaved herself and her lump out of the chair.

On the doorstep stood two men, but no Kate.

'Oh.' Dawn was really worried now. 'I thought you were my sister.'

'Actually, we're police officers,' said one of the men, holding up his identification card.

'What?' said Dawn, faintly.

They were Detective Sergeant something, and Detective Constable something else, and they wanted to come in. Dawn was terrified. 'You can't, my mum's not home.'

'Well, it's not your mum we're looking for, love. It's a Frank Hodges, I believe he lives here.'

'No! No, he doesn't, he doesn't.'

'Our information says he does.'

'Well he used to, but he doesn't now.' Was that the right thing to say? Dawn twisted her hands together, trying to think.

'It's perishing out here,' Detective Sergeant something pointed out. 'And you can bet the neighbours are listening!'

Trembling, Dawn let the police officers in.

In the sitting room, Dad was white-faced and round eyed. 'Nothing to do with us! Frank Hodges ain't nothing to do with our family. Been gone a long time.'

'How long is long?'

Dad began to cough. The hacking went on and on. 'That's a nasty chest, sir,' said Detective Constable something.

'I ain't supposed to get cold.' (*Hack, hack, hack*). 'And I ain't supposed to get upset.' (*Hack, hack, hack* again).

'Won't keep you long, sir. Just wondering if you can tell us where Frank Hodges was on the afternoon of the ninth.'

'The ninth?'

'February the ninth. Monday. This Monday just past.'

'*Monday*?' said Dawn, bewildered. 'That's the day Mrs Harris's house got burgled.'

'It is.'

'Frank never done that, somebody else done that!'

Was *that* the wrong thing to say? Dawn bit her lip and hoped she hadn't blundered.

'Actually, it's not that burglary we're investigating.'

'Oh.'

'There were two break-ins that afternoon. Wessex Road, and over in Rushmore Gardens.'

'Oh.'

'We have reason to believe that Frank Hodges can help us in the Rushmore Gardens one.... Sorry, love – your husband, isn't it?'

Help them, Dawn thought, in terror. They mean Frank did it! *Helping the police with their enquiries* – that's what they say when they're trying to make someone confess. She opened her mouth, and blurted the words out. 'It wasn't Frank, it was Spotted Dick!'

'Oh, we know all about *him*,' said the policeman. 'As a matter of fact we've already got him. *And* the van he was obliging enough to smash up for us to find.'

'*Oh*,' Dawn whispered.

'And we know he had a mate with him,' the policeman went on, without mercy. 'Spotty Dick, that is – we know he had a mate with him. And, well, that's where we think Frank could help us!'

'It couldn't be Frank!' Dawn declared, bravely. 'He was here all day.'

'No he wasn't,' said Dad.

'He was. He was!'

'You're thinking of another Monday!'

'I'm thinking of *this* Monday!' Dawn's voice was rising with hysteria. '*Dad*!'

'We're not shielding no criminals in this house,' said Dad. 'We're law-abiding in this house.'

'DAD!' Dawn screamed at him.

'What's the matter with you, Dawnie? You want Mr Duffy to think we shield criminals? You want that?'

He began to cough once more. He coughed, and his face went red, and the veins stood out pitifully on his neck. Detective Sergeant something tried to say 'Shall we start again' but his words were quite drowned out by the sound of Dad's coughing.

That's right, you traitor, Dawn thought viciously, you cough! You cough yourself sick, go on! The least you can do now is use your coughing to stop these horrible policemen from making us answer any more questions. These crafty policemen that are too sly even to *dress* like proper policemen. Go on, you keep up that coughing till Mum comes home. . . . and please, Mum, come quick! Come quick, and sort out this mess for me.

Oh, Mum, come QUICK!

Kate had retreated amongst the tombstones again, away from the railings. She was chilled through now, and shaking. Desmond took off his own coat, and put it round the heap that was Kate. She jerked away from his touch, and the anorak half fell off. Desmond picked it up, and put it round her shoulders once more. He had no idea how long they had been there, but it seemed like hours. He had coaxed, and coaxed, and still she had not spoken one word. He tried again. 'Come on, Kate. Come on, let's go home, eh?'

She muttered something then, and Desmond bent to catch the words. 'Say it again. Come on Kate. Say it again, I didn't hear.'

'I said I thought we was locked in anyway.' The words were mumbled, but just audible.

'Well, we are, but the railings ain't all that high!' said Desmond, eagerly. 'They ain't high, Kate. We could climb over!'

Silence.

'We could climb over. I'll help you. Come on!'

'. . . No.' Her voice was strained, remote.

'But why not? We can't stay here all night!'

'. . . I can.'

'You can't! You going to freeze to death!'

'That's what I want to do.'

'KATE!'

'It's all right. This cemetery is meant for dead people. I will be just another dead person, in this cemetery.'

'You're mad! At last it really happened, you've gone mad!'

'Actually, I don't care. I finished caring.'

'Well, *I* haven't! *I* haven't finished caring!'

'You climb over the railings then, and go home,' said Kate, in her faraway voice.

'I mean I haven't finished caring about you, you crazy mad person. . . . Crazy! You're crazy!'

Tripping and stumbling in the dark, Desmond ran back to the railings. The huge flats beyond reached into a padded, grey-black sky. There were lights in the windows, and Desmond began to shout for help; but the fog muffled his voice, and no one seemed to hear. In his desperation, he even thought of climbing the railings and going to look for a policeman – but he was frightened to leave Kate alone so long. What mad thing might she do when he was gone? She was out of her mind, and she made him think of something only he didn't know

224

what it was. . . . Yes he did, it was one of those glass ornaments on the shelf at home. Kate was like that – brittle, and easy to break. If somebody didn't look out for her she could get smashed up, into little pieces.

Tripping and stumbling again, Desmond ran back and was relieved to find Kate still safely huddled under his coat.

'I thought you went home. Why didn't you go home?' She didn't seem bothered, either way.

'Why do you think?' said Desmond, savagely. 'I can't leave you by yourself, can I! You crazy, mad, raving, loony, bonkers person!'

He stamped, and swung his arms in the raw and biting air. Much longer like this, and they would both freeze anyway. Perhaps he would have to go for help after all. What did he ought to do, what did he ought to do?

There was a sort of idea, at the back of his mind, about how he might persuade her; but it was only a glimmer, and complicated besides. The cold clutched at Desmond's thinking as he struggled with his idea, trying desperately to see it whole and clear.

'You're wasting your time,' said Mum. 'I don't know what Frank was doing Monday, and I haven't got the least interest.'

'Your daughter says he was in the house,' said Detective Constable something.

'Well, she says wrong.'

'Where is he now?'

'Don't ask me!'

'Mrs Hodges?' said the policeman to Dawn.

'She don't know neither,' said Mum.

'Mr Jackson?'

'Nor him,' said Mum.

'You sure Frank Hodges didn't leave an address?'

'How many times am I supposed to repeat myself?'

'Actually, he went to South America,' said Dawn.

'Shut your stupid face!' said Mum.

'Kate,' said Desmond. 'Are you listening, I got something to say.'

Silence.

'You're upset about that thing Frank said, aren't you? About he doesn't love Dawn any more. And about he push you out.'

No answer.

'But the thing is, the thing is, Kate, I think he told a lie!'

'. . . What you mean?'

Encouraged by even this tiny response, Desmond pressed on. 'I think he just said that because of who was listening.'

Silence, again. Her head was turned from him, but he could sense the small quiver of attention.

'I think that was his story. About breaking up with Dawn, I think that was Frank's story. You know, for his dad, and his stepmum, and his stepmum's mum. I think he didn't tell them he was running from the police, and your mum throw him out. I think he said he broke up with Dawn instead. . . . Get it?'

Kate sat up slowly.

'Get it?' said Desmond, again.

'. . . I don't know.'

'Well, anyway, that's what I think. I think he said those things because he was scared. He was

226

like scared you would let it out what really happened. He's a scaredy-cat, ain't he. What a creep!'

Silence.

'I reckon he loves Dawn all the time, only he's scared to say it. Don't you think that? Now?'

'I don't know, I don't know.'

'You don't want to freeze to death any more though, do you? You don't want to do that, Kate, do you? Come on – say you don't want to do that any more!'

Kate got up and began to run, blindly, towards the railings. 'What you doing?' Desmond's anorak had fallen on to the grass, but he didn't wait to pick it up. What crazy thing was Kate up to now? Desmond pounded after her.

She was trying to climb. 'Wait! Let me help you!'

Kate clutched frantically at the fence. 'I have to get home! I have to get home before my mum finds out!'

Desmond did not point out that it was far too late for that. 'Let me help you, though. You'll hurt yourself!' He put his hands under her, and pushed. 'Mind the spikes!'

They should have planned it properly. All excited like that she would never do it! But somehow in her frenzy she did. Somehow, with Desmond taking her weight, she scrabbled to the top of the fence and crouched there, her hands holding tightly to the spikes on either side of her.

'Now wait for me!' He meant that she should wait for him to help her down from the other side – but Kate could not wait! Dismayed, Desmond saw the dark silhouette of her straighten up, sway on top of the spikes . . . and then lurch forward as she jumped, wildly and clumsily, to the ground.

* * *

'Cheerio!' said Mum, banging the door behind the police officers. 'Nice to see you, don't come again!'

'*Right*!' said Dad, fervently.

'Best see about something to eat, then,' said Mum. 'Come on, Dawn! You can get off your backside and help me, for once. And pull yourself together, spineless! They've gone, haven't they?'

15

The end of the road

'Are you all right?' said Desmond. He had followed Kate over the railings, as fast as he could. She still lay as she had fallen, curled up on the ground. Desmond peered down anxiously at the scarcely moving heap.

'I don't know,' said Kate. 'My foot hurts.'

'Can you stand up?'

With the aid of the railings, Kate hauled herself on to one leg. But when she tried to touch the other foot to the ground, she gave a yell. 'It *hurts*! It got all twisted over when I fell.'

'You didn't ought to have jumped like that. If you would have let me lift you down, you wouldn't have hurt yourself.'

'I know.' There was shame in her voice. 'I think I went a bit funny back there. In the cemetery. I think I went a bit peculiar. It's all right, I finished that now. The only thing is, now my foot is too sore to stand on.'

'So you can't walk?'

'No.'

Desmond pondered. 'Well, that's it, then. I shall have to get some help. I shall have to go to that police station. They got plenty cars there – they can take us home. The police do good things like that sometimes, you know,' he said, grudgingly.

'No, not the police, not the police!'

'Well I don't like the police neither, really. But the thing is, I can't think of anything else.'

'I can hop! Look, I can hop!' Kate made one small, valiant leap, and clutched at the railings again, biting her lip.

'You can't do it, can you!'

'Something happened to the other one as well,' she admitted. 'When I jumped on it.' She sat down slowly and carefully, her face twisted with pain, her hands round the badly sprained ankle. 'I know, I could crawl! On my hands and knees.'

'Don't be stupid!'

Kate began to cry. 'I don't know what to do! It's all gone wrong! Everything has gone wrong up to now – well, nearly everything – and it's getting more wrong all the time, and I don't know what's going to happen, and I don't know what to do. . . . And I'm *thirsty*,' she added, as though that were the final straw.

'There was some orange juice left.'

'I don't know where my bag is. My bag is in the cemetery, I think. . . . And Dawn's letter.'

'Well, we're not going back there!'

'I know. . . . My glasses fell off, as well.'

'We're not going back for your glasses, neither. I best get the police, Kate. Eh?'

'No, no, no! They will ask questions. They will ask why we come here.' Her voice was rising in pitch. 'They will find out about Frank, and put him in prison.' She gulped, hysterically; she was clearly terrified. 'Not the police, Desmond, *please!*'

He pondered, poking at the broken tooth. '. . . All right, I'll carry you.'

She was afraid to believe it. 'Will you?'

'Yep.'

230

'All the way to the station?'

'Yep.'

'You can't, though, I'm too heavy.'

'You ain't heavy!' said Desmond, scornfully. 'You don't weigh so much as a feather!'

But when he had her on his back, with her arms tightly round his neck, he found she was a great deal heavier than she looked. He took a few staggering paces. 'Not past the police station though, Desmond, *please*!' Kate begged.

'All right, all right, I'll find another way.'

He stumbled a few steps in the opposite direction. 'I *am* a bit heavy, aren't I?' said Kate, in a small voice.

'I said you're not heavy and you're not! Don't go on about it, Frog!'

Desmond pushed on, through the thick blanket of fog. The school bag and the glasses were not the only things that had got left behind in the cemetery. There was Desmond's anorak as well – and he was cold, *so* cold without his anorak. Not to mention the fact that he was going to be in deep trouble at home for losing it. Anyway, it would be nice and warm on the train. Desmond filled his mind with thoughts of the warm train, as he looked for another way to get to the station.

He found a turning through some more flats. The road twisted and branched, and Desmond could not be at all sure he was following the right path. Where was the main road, where was it? He couldn't hear any traffic.

His knees began to buckle.

'Put me down,' said Kate. 'Have a rest.'

'Belt up!'

He pushed on, clenching his teeth. Right foot,

left foot, right foot again. And I wish my legs were not so wobbly, Desmond thought. But I'm not going to stop for a rest, because if I do that Kate will think I'm not strong.

Anyway, I bet I'm stronger that Curtis. I bet Curtis's legs would be a lot more wobblier than mine. I bet Matthew's legs would be more wobblier, as well. And Ashraf's. Ashraf couldn't carry a baby even, I don't think. I can carry a heavy person all this way because I'm strong. I'm probably the strongest person in the class. I wish the boys in the class could see me now, only not really because they would say those silly things. I am strong, though – look how strong I am!

He exulted in the thought. He felt the thought swelling inside him, making itself come true. If he could only just find the station. . . .

I wish I was on the train already, he thought. I wish Kate was sitting beside of me, instead of all heavy on my back.

It's going to be lovely and warm, in the train.

. . . How will I get Kate down those steps?

. . . Good job we got the return tickets, so I don't have to think about getting past·the ticket man without paying.

Good job we got the tickets!

. . . *Have* we got the tickets, though?

Kate was looking after them. She bought them with her money, and she was looking after them . . . I didn't see where she put them, but it was most likely in her school bag. And her school bag is in the cemetery! It's back in the cemetery, in the graves somewhere!

. . . Perhaps she has some more money, enough

to buy some more tickets. Only that will most likely be in her school bag as well.

How are we going to manage?

'What's the matter?' said Kate anxiously, on Desmond's back.

'Nothing,' said Desmond. 'There's nothing the matter.'

He clung to a lamp-post, because his knees were suddenly weak again. Now his arms were no longer supporting her legs, the whole of Kate's weight hung from his neck. Never mind the police station, they should have gone by the road! It was too far this way; it was too much, he couldn't stand it!

'I *knew* I was too heavy,' said Kate.

There was a desperate sadness in her voice, and Desmond couldn't stand *that*. It's the most important thing in the world for her, he thought. To get home, without the police seeing her, that's the most important thing in the world for Kate. And it's all up to me, and I *like* it to be all up to me. . . . *And I'm going to do it, so there.*

He grasped Kate's legs, and took a deep breath.

Moments later, he found himself staggering into the main road.

They were nearly there all the time! Just when he was thinking they weren't going to make it, they were really almost there! Light-headed with relief and triumph, Desmond turned towards the station, which surely could not be far now. If it were not for the fog he would be able to see it, probably.

'Desmond, I think you're great!' Kate's voice rang with joy. 'We will need the tickets now, won't we? For the train.'

'Don't worry about the tickets, Kate. Don't you

worry about the tickets. It's my problem about the tickets.'

'It's me that's got to get them out, though,' said Kate. 'The tickets are in my pocket.'

'Whoopee!' Desmond grinned, baring the broken tooth. There was nothing left to worry about now, nothing at all! He could manage the rest, easy peasy! So he laughed, and whooped, and collapsed against a wall – sliding carefully to the ground because the truth was, for the moment, the strongest person in the class couldn't actually hold Kate any longer. And Kate laughed a bit too, out of politeness to this person who had done so much for her today – though she couldn't see, herself, that anything was exactly *funny*.

'Let's have a little rest,' said Desmond. Every bit of him ached. He didn't think he had ached so much in his life, ever before. 'Only a *little* rest. I'm only a *little* bit tired, you know.'

Grunting with pain, Kate eased herself off Desmond's back, and the children sat side by side on the pavement. They sat away from the street lights, in a nice thick patch of fog, though in any case the road was almost deserted. 'I'm c-cold,' said Kate.

'So am I. Sit closer.'

Good job Curtis couldn't see him now! Desmond put a protective arm round Kate while he could, while there was no one to see, and misunderstand. There was a strong sort of feeling in his chest, a good feeling. It was great to have someone depend on you, it was really great. It made you feel like a giant, sort of.

'Are you going to carry me down the steps, Desmond?' said Kate.

'Yep. In a minute.'

'Are you going to carry me on the train?'

'Yep.'

'People will think it's funny. What if they ask?'

'I shall tell them to mind their own business. Just leave it to me.' He was bursting with confidence now. What a fabulous day this was turning out to be!

'Are you going to carry me all the way to my house?' said Kate.

'Course I am. What you keep asking for?'

'Desmond,' said Kate. 'I think you're *wonderful*!'

'Oh, belt up! It's no big deal!'

Yes, it *had* been a very good day. The best one in his life so far, probably.

'Did you know Kate ain't back yet?' said Dad, actually making a special journey into the kitchen to say it.

'Back from where?' said Mum.

'She ain't come home from school.'

'*What*? I thought she was hiding from the police. In the bedroom or something.'

'She ain't come home from school, though,' said Dad, again. 'I mean, she didn't ought to worry us like this, did she?'

'Something must have happened! Look – it's nearly quarter to seven!'

'She's probably round Suzette's,' said Dawn, playing desperately for time.

'I'll have the hide off of her if she is!' said Mum. 'All this time, without letting us know. Anyway, I don't believe it, when did she ever? Go on up to the phone box then, Dawn. Ring Suzette's mum.'

'It's cold!' Dawn pleaded. 'And the phone box is mostly out of order. And I keep getting this pain.'

'All right, call up to old Duffy. Ask if we can have a lend of his phone.'

'No, Dawnie, not that,' said Dad anxiously. 'You go up the phone box, like your mum said.'

'There's no need to make all that fuss to phone,' said Dawn. 'She's sure to be in soon, sure to.'

Mum looked hard and long at Dawn. 'You know something, don't you?'

'No!'

'Yes you do, it's written all over your face. Come on, where is she?'

Dawn, already shattered by the visit of the police, began to shake. 'What are you hiding?' said Mum.

'Nothing.'

'Don't come that with me!'

Dawn burst into tears.

'And you can turn off the waterworks!' said Mum. 'Now. Where's Kate?'

'She went to Bow, to look for Frank. At his dad's.'

'Oh, she did, did she? I suppose you put her up to it!'

'Dawnie!' said Dad, aghast.

'I didn't know about the other burglary. I didn't know that then. I didn't know Frank was guilty all the time.'

'You won't listen to me, will you? I told you he was scared out of his pants! I'm not a bit surprised he done another burglary. He probably done a dozen more burglaries. But of course, you wouldn't listen to *me*.'

'Yeah, but I thought—'

'I should stop thinking if I was you,' said Mum.

'Because you don't know how to think straight.
How long has Kate been gone?'

'All day.'

'*All day?*'

'I didn't mean anything bad to happen to Kate,'
said Dawn, piteously.

'Didn't *mean*, didn't *mean*, what's *mean* got to do
with it? . . . All right, don't answer, just tell me
where she went. Exactly.'

'I don't know the address.'

'You sent Kate all the way to Bow by herself,
and you don't even know the address?'

'She wasn't by herself. Desmond went with
her . . . I think.'

'I don't believe this! You sent Kate off to Bow
with that little scum-bag, you *think*?'

Dawn doubled up and clutched her stomach.
'I've got a pain.'

'Shut up about your pain! We haven't got time
for your pain now. . . . Is he on the phone?'

'Do you mean Frank's dad?'

'No, no, I mean Father Christmas!'

'I don't know,' said Dawn. 'He could be. Yeah,
I think he is.'

'You great useless pudding! Why didn't you look
in the book and find out?'

'I don't know. I didn't think of phoning. I made
a nice card for Kate to take.'

'Oh, really? I didn't know you was still in the
Infants' School!'

'*And* a letter,' said Dawn. 'I didn't think of
phoning.'

'But the *address*, Mastermind! Why didn't you
look in the phone book to find the address?'

237

'I didn't think of it. I knew the name of the road
– nearly.'

'What do you mean *nearly*?'

'I told Kate Benfield Road, but really it's *Den*field
Road. I remembered it properly after she went.'

'That's handy,' said Mum. 'That's really handy!'

'She could have found it, though. Somebody
could have put her right. She could be there now.
They could have asked her in to tea.'

'Do me a favour!'

'They could have! They asked me once!'

'Very likely. Would you have stayed all this time
if you had me to answer to when you come back?'

'Oh, yeah,' said Dawn, wretchedly. 'But what
could have happened? I can't think what could have
happened. I can't, Mum.'

'Oh, yes you can! You watch the News same as
me! . . . Now just get upstairs and ask old Duffy if
we can borrow his phone book a minute.'

'What's wrong with the phone box one?' asked
Dad.

'Who asked you?'

'I keep getting this pain,' said Dawn.

'Very convenient,' said Mum. 'Now go up and
get the phone book, like I said.'

Dawn went up the stairs slowly. She stopped
halfway, and held on to the banister.

'Go on!' said Mum. 'What you waiting for?'

Dawn sat on the stair with her arms round her
lump, rocking backwards and forwards. Her eyes
were wide with apprehension. Mum looked at her
sharply. 'Oh no! Trust you!'

'Is she having the baby?' said Dad, anxiously.

'No, no, she's having an elephant. No kidding, I

think she really is having it this time. Cheer up, Dawn, soon be over!'

'It's not the right time,' Dad protested. 'It's not supposed to be yet.'

'Explain that to the baby.'

'The hospital, though, the hospital!' Dad's voice croaked with agitation. 'She has to get to the hospital!'

At the mention of that word, Dawn began to wail. 'I'm scared. I'm scared!'

'Oh, stop that noise. I'm coming with you!' said Mum, tartly. 'Don't think I'm leaving you to go through it on your own do you, you poor silly cow? Come on, let's get your things together.'

'What about Kate?' Poor Dad, he had so many fears now, he didn't know which one to be most afraid of. 'You're not leaving me to deal with that on my own, are you?'

Mum looked at Dad, and passed a weary arm over her forehead. Her face was tight with strain. 'Oh, I'm not messing about no more. I'm getting the police.'

'Not *yet*!' said Dad, in fresh alarm.

'When then? After she been missing a couple more hours? Out in this lovely weather? If not something worse!'

'Not the *police*, though, Mum!' Dawn's wails broke out afresh.

'Don't you start.'

'You won't tell them Frank's address, though, will you? You won't tell them that!'

'No use giving 'em half a story. They got to know where to begin looking.'

'*Mum*! Where you *going*?'

'Where d'you think I'm going? Upstairs of

239

course, to ask Mr Duffy for a lend of his phone!
Police first, then a taxi for you, Madam.'

'No, Mum, don't do it! Don't do it, *please*! Please,
Mum, don't tell on Frank!'

'Shut your face!' said Mum furiously, from the
sixth step up. 'My child's safety comes first, and
I'm not taking no chances with that . . . not for a
million Franks!'

'Desmond,' said Kate, on the train. 'Do you think
God is on our side now?'

'I dunno.'

'*I* think he is. It's all going right, now. I think
God is going to tell the angels to keep the police
away from us, all the way to my house. So they
won't have to find out about Frank, and put him
in prison.'

'Oh.' Did he really want any interfering angels
pushing their noses into his business? After his successful day, Desmond was not at all sure about that.

Kate was conscious of a fierce throbbing pain
in her ankle. Her shoe felt tight, but she was
afraid that if she took it off she wouldn't get it
on again. Nevertheless, she was strangely happy.
'Desmond—'

'What?'

'You *are* my friend, aren't you?'

'Yep.'

'Are you going to be my friend for ever, now?'

'Yeah, I suppose so.'

'Because otherwise I only got Suzette. And she
isn't really much good.'

'Yeah. . . . There is one problem, though.'

'You mean those silly things they're saying about
us?' said Kate, anxiously.

240

'No, not that, something else.' Desmond shifted uncomfortably. 'I forgot to mention it.'

'Mention what?'

'We're moving. Our family is going to move soon. We're going to Birmingham to live.'

'Oh, *no*!'

'We are, though. It's because of my dad. He couldn't get a job nowhere round here. See, my uncle's got a garage, and he repairs cars, and my dad's going to work for him. My dad's brilliant at things like that,' said Desmond, with pride.

'Oh.'

'I got a lot of uncles and aunties in Birmingham. And cousins. It's going to be good!'

'Oh.'

'I could write to you. I could write you a letter.'

'You won't! You won't do it!'

Maybe she was right, thought Desmond. He never had liked writing, much. He would think about it, though.

'It's not fair!' said Kate, bitterly. 'They take everything away!'

Desmond said nothing. What was there to say?

'Everything! They take everything away from me! It's not fair!'

16

And round the corner

In the early hours of the morning, Mum came back. Kate had been sleeping the sleep of exhaustion, but she woke up when Mum banged the front door. 'Kate's home,' said Dad.

'I know,' said Mum. 'Is she all right?'

'Oh, it's all been happening here, wait till I tell you! First the police come round this house; then they went round them Lockes'; then—'

'I know all about that! Phoned the police from the hospital, didn't I? I said is Kate all right?'

'*She's* all right. Am *I* all right, though?' [*cough, cough, cough.*] 'I had to deal with everything, you know. The police and everything. All by myself.'

'Shut up about yourself! I'll try again. Is *Kate* all right?'

'Only sprained her ankle. . . . I think it's only a sprain. . . . Oh yeah, and she's a bit upset. Keeps on about it's all her fault Frank's going to get arrested. Keeps on about it, gets on your nerves!'

'Ah – she'll get over it,' said Mum.

'I made her a cup of tea. I said "I best make this cup of tea while we still got a kitchen for me to make it *in*." How's Dawn getting on, then?'

'Wait a minute.' Mum opened the door of the back bedroom. Lying in bed, Kate trembled. *Now* it was coming! Now the world was going to come crashing down around her ears – the bit of the world that hadn't crashed down already!

242

'Are you awake . . . *Aunty*?' Mum didn't sound cross at all, she sounded happy.

'*Aunty*?' said Dad.

'That's right . . . *Grandpa*,' said Mum.

Kate sat up in bed, and tried to still the clamour in her head. 'Mum—'

'Call me Grandma,' said Mum, with a grin that stretched from ear to ear.

'Is Mr Duffy really going to throw us out, then?' said Kate.

'Nah!' said Mum. 'I don't think he hardly took any of it in, in the end.'

'They did arrest Frank, though.'

'He had it coming.'

'I know. He broke his promise after all, didn't he? But I think he only done it for Dawn. He does love Dawn, you know, he does *really* . . . It must be really horrible in prison.'

'Do him good. Teach him a lesson. You're too forgiving, Kate.'

'It was my fault, though,' said Kate, remorsefully. 'It was all because of me Frank got arrested.'

'It wasn't your fault, and don't you go on thinking no such rubbish! Do you hear me? I don't want to hear no more about it was your fault! It was Lady Muck's fault with her great ideas, and Frank's with his lies, that's whose fault it was.'

'Do you think Frank will be in prison for a long time? Will he be there for years and years?'

'Nah – first offence, innit. Be out just in time for going into that new place I reckon. The rate this council is getting on with finding it.'

'Will Dawn and Frank go back together, then?'

'If they don't they'll have me to answer to! They

243

got responsibilities now, you know. Have to grow up some time. Both of them.'

She had changed her tune a bit from before, but that was not unusual. You never knew which way Mum was going to go. Kate put a piece of hair into her mouth, and chewed it sadly. 'I think everybody has got something to look forward to now, excepting me!' She thought again about Desmond and how much she was going to miss him.

'Cheer up,' said Mum. 'You never know what's round the corner!'

Dawn was home, with baby Gemma. Dawn sat on the edge of the bed and fed Gemma, her face glowing with pride. Kate watched, entranced. 'Can I change her now?' she begged. '*Please*, Dawn! Let me change her!'

'I don't mind,' said Dawn, graciously.

Handling the tiny body with reverence, Kate swabbed and wrapped as she had seen Dawn do before. She put her finger into the baby's hand, and her heart overflowed as she felt the minuscule fingers curling round. 'She *likes* me,' said Kate, in wonder. 'Do you know something, Dawn? I think Gemma likes me to change her!'

'Do you want to do it every time, then?'

'*Can* I?' said Kate, with shining eyes.

'You can do it in the night as well, if you like. When she yells. We'll share it – all right? I'll feed her and you change her. All right?'

'Oh, *thank* you!' Kate breathed.

There was a new girl in Kate's seat.

Kate had been away for two weeks. The first week it was half term anyway. The second week

Kate insisted that her foot was still too sore for limping to school on. At the beginning of the third week, Mum's patience ran out. 'Come on, you got to face it some time!'

'They'll laugh at me! They'll tease me!'

'I don't see why. I don't see why they have to know anything about it. *I* haven't told them nothing. All I told them was you got a sprained ankle.'

So Kate dragged to school, not wanting to, and late. It was a dismal sort of day, with a gusty wind and rain clouds heavy in the sky. In the classroom, the smell of wet shoes mingled with the smell of pencil shavings.

And there was somebody else in Kate's seat.

'Frog's back,' said Natasha. 'That well known loony.'

'I beg your pardon!' said Mrs Warren.

Mrs Warren was fatter than ever. She was bursting out of the tight green jumper, but she was smiling, and her eyes were warm for Kate. 'Come along, Kate, we'll put an extra table, and make a bigger group. This is Francine, by the way. I've an idea you two have something in common!'

Kate squinted sideways at Francine, and Francine squinted sideways at Kate. 'What's that you're reading?' said Kate.

'It's called *Go Ahead Secret Seven*.'

'*I* like the Secret Seven books.'

'Do you!' Francine's cheeks were pink with pleasure.

'Yes, I do.' Kate's cheeks were pink with pleasure as well.

'I think they're great.'

'*I* think they're great, too.' There had been a

reason, a long time ago, why she went off the Secret Seven, but for the moment Kate couldn't remember what it was. 'Do you want a sweet?' she said to the new girl.

Francine beamed at Kate, and Kate beamed at Francine. Happiness sparked between them. With their heads close, they read the book together.

Other great reads from **Red Fox**

Further Red Fox titles that you might enjoy reading are listed on the following pages. They are available in bookshops or they can be ordered directly from us.

   If you would like to order books, please send this form and the money due to:

ARROW BOOKS, BOOKSERVICE BY POST, PO BOX 29, DOUGLAS, ISLE OF MAN, BRITISH ISLES. Please enclose a cheque or postal order made out to Arrow Books Ltd for the amount due, plus 75p per book for postage and packing to a maximum of £7.50, both for orders within the UK. For customers outside the UK, please allow £1.00 per book.

NAME_____

ADDRESS_____

_____

Please print clearly.

Whilst every effort is made to keep prices low, it is sometimes necessary to increase cover prices at short notice. If you are ordering books by post, to save delay it is advisable to phone to confirm the correct price. The number to ring is THE SALES DEPARTMENT 071 (if outside London) 973 9700.

Other great reads from **Red Fox**

Leap into humour and adventure with Joan Aiken

Joan Aiken writes wild adventure stories laced with comedy and melodrama that have made her one of the best-known writers today. Her James III series, which begins with *The Wolves of Willoughby Chase*, has been recognized as a modern classic. Packed with action from beginning to end, her books are a wild romp through a history that never happened.

THE WOLVES OF WILLOUGHBY CHASE
ISBN 0 09 997250 6 £2.99

BLACK HEARTS IN BATTERSEA
ISBN 0 09 988860 2 £3.50

NIGHT BIRDS ON NANTUCKET
ISBN 0 09 988890 4 £3.50

THE STOLEN LAKE
ISBN 0 09 988840 8 £3.50

THE CUCKOO TREE
ISBN 0 09 988870 X £3.50

DIDO AND PA
ISBN 0 09 988850 5 £3.50

IS
ISBN 0 09 910921 2 £2.99

THE WHISPERING MOUNTAIN
ISBN 0 09 988830 0 £3.50

MIDNIGHT IS A PLACE
ISBN 0 09 979200 1 £3.50

THE SHADOW GUESTS
ISBN 0 09 988820 3 £2.99

Other great reads from **Red Fox**

Gripping reads by Ruth Thomas

Guilty

Kate is thrilled by the local burglary until playground gossip points the finger at her friend Desmond's father who has recently come out of prison. Kate and Desmond set out together to discover who really is . . . GUILTY!

ISBN 0 09 918519 1   £2.99

The Runaways
Winner of the Guardian Fiction Award

Teachers and parents are suspicious when Julia and Nathan start flashing around the stash of money they found in a deserted house. There's only one way out – to run away . . .

ISBN 0 09 959660 1   £2.99

The New Boy

Donovan is the new boy in the class – secretive, brooding and mysterious. At first Amy is flattered that he wants her to be his friend – until he pushes the limit of her loyalty to the extreme.

ISBN 0 09 973410 9   £2.99

The Secret

When Mum fails to return from her weekend away, Nicky and Roy resolve not to let on to anyone that their mother has abandoned them.

ISBN 0 09 984000 6   £2.99

The Class that Went Wild

Ever since Mrs Lloyd left to have a baby, Class 4L has been impossible! Sean and the gang just get rowdier and rowdier, and even Gillian's twin brother Joseph joins in. Gillian tries to save the situation, but then Joseph goes missing . . .

ISBN 0 09 963210 1   £2.99